Paint the Devil

The Wolf in Denmark

by Christoffer Petersen

Paint the Devil

Published by Aarluuk Press

Original Cover Image: Gregoire Bertrand (Unsplash)

ISBN: 978-87-93680-10-4

www.christoffer-petersen.com

PAINT THE DEVIL

At male fanden på væggen

A Danish saying translated as

To paint the Devil on the wall

meaning

to imagine or fear the worst.

Only the mountain has lived long enough to listen
objectively to the howl of the wolf.

— Aldo Leopold (1887-1948)

from

A Sand County Almanac:
And Sketches Here and There

A shepherd never forgets his sheep,
that run along the wild beat,
where the wolf lies in cover;
the ninety-nine must do their best
in the desert, and the dust;
the lost will he gather.

Author's translation from
En hyrde glemmer fåret ej
from
Luke 15:1-10
Lorenz Lorenzen 1700
Hans Adolph Brorson 1735

En hyrde glemmer fåret ej,
som løber på den vilde vej,
hvor ulven er at vente;
ni og halvfemsindstyve må
det, som det kan, i ørken gå;
det tabte vil han hente.

Introduction

I was living and working in Qaanaaq, Greenland, roughly 800 miles from the North Pole, when I heard about the wolf in Denmark. It was 2012, and a body of a wolf had been found in the Hanstholm Nature Reserve in Thy, in Jutland. Prior to the wolf in Thy, the last wild wolf in Denmark was recorded in 1813, over 199 years ago. I was living in one of the wildest and most extreme places in the world, yet one of the animals I find most fascinating was in Denmark, the smallest and flattest of the Scandinavian countries. Small, flat, and full of deer – a perfect habitat for the Grey Wolf. I joked with my brother-in-law that if they ever found a live wolf, we would return to Denmark. A year later we moved back to Jutland and rented a small flat in wolf country.

What struck me most about the return of the wolf was the way it split the nation between those who loved the idea of wild wolves in Denmark, and those who hated it – not just the idea, they hated the wolf. But why? Was it out of fear, ignorance, concern? Did hunters hate the wolf because it threatened their interests? Parents because they were frightened for the safety of their children? Did pet-owners worry that cats and dogs would be carried off in the night, and did farmers have just cause to worry about their livestock?

Given the geographical size of Denmark, about six times smaller than the United Kingdom, wolves will often range close to small villages and towns, cross farmland, and likely share the same paths and trails through forests and nature reserves as humans. There are plenty of good arguments suggesting that the wolf does not belong in Denmark.

Not today.

Not ever.

But it is here, and the first cubs were born in Denmark in 2018. In the same year, the first wolf was illegally shot and killed in Denmark. Facebook groups and pages were swamped with emotionally-charged comments and I discovered a new side of people I thought I once knew, people that shared the same views of nature that I did. All of a sudden, on the subject of wolves, we were poles apart.

The idea and the *need* to do something, *anything*, bothered me for some time, so I hit the books, the media – print and social, and pulled together the ideas for *Paint the Devil*, teased them into a story, and then let the words flow.

Paint the Devil is a work of fiction influenced by the intense debate and the heat of the summer of 2018.

The summer of the wolf.

Chris
October 2018
Denmark

PAINT THE
DEVIL

199 years to return to Denmark
6 years to divide the country

Chapter 1

The ground crumbles beneath stunted yellow grass, as Bo Falk shines the beam of his halogen lamp across the field. It's over thirty degrees Celsius in the day, twenty at night, making the carcass of the dead ewe bloat in the heat. He clicks the lamp off and on again, seeing first one beast, then another, capturing what he knows to be the predatory gaze of the wolf. This is the pair he has heard about, the wolves rumoured to have made their den somewhere in the woods, between the Falk family farm and his neighbours'. Bo watches the wolves as they watch him, and then he shouts at them, the law says that's all he can do.

"Bugger off, you evil brutes. The devil take you. This is my land. *Mine.*"

Bo kicks at the dusty surface of his field, cursing the land as he curses the wolves. There's no fodder. He's already exceeded the summer budget, piling on the debt until the money is nothing but numbers and the bank pumps more money into Bo Falk, money for feed, money for water. Falk men and women have farmed this land for six generations, and now there is only debt to pass to his son, and more debt that his son will pass on to his children. Last year it was unseasonably wet, this year a drought, and now the wolf.

Bo hurls the trigger lamp across the field, hears it crash on the dry earth beyond the carcass, pulls out his phone as the light disappears with the splinter of glass, and strides across the dead grass to his dead sheep. The wolves are gone.

"Bo?" his wife calls, peering into the darkness, her t-shirt clinging damp to her skin, her hair, slick with sweat, sticking to her cheeks, her forehead, her shoulders. "What is it?"

"Wolves," he says. "I'm calling Viktoria."

"Now? It's three in the morning."

"Yes, now. Get Jacob up."

"He's asleep, Bo."

"He needs to see this."

"Can't he see it in the morning?"

He ignores her and she hears him bark something at the farm veterinarian. If she drives now, she'll be at the Falk farm in just twenty minutes, long before first light. *If* she leaves now. Camilla Falk isn't so sure, not about that, and not about the wolves. But if Bo says it is wolves, she believes him.

Camilla walks back to the farmhouse, her heels rubbing inside the leather boots, the soles slap slapping on the cobbles, dragging dust from the dry paddock. The crickets rub frantic legs together and she is distracted as she tries to remember the last time there were so many. Not last year, last year was too wet.

"And now too dry," she says, her last thought on the crickets as she unlatches the door to the main house. Falk farm lies just four kilometres outside the village of Thyrup, West Jutland, just a spit and a strong gust of wind to the sea, the broad beaches, the tourist traps of the Danish west coast. Camilla kicks off the boots, pads through the stone-flagged kitchen and along the short corridor, past the painting of the church cross on the hillside to Jacob's room. He's sleeping, legs sprawled over the rumpled bed sheet, duvet on the floor, window open. She enters the room, presses a small hand on his bare shoulder, shakes him gently and whispers him awake.

"It's not even dawn," he mumbles, his mouth thick with warm air, eyes gritty with sleep.

"Your father wants you."

"Now?"

"A sheep is dead. One of the ewes. You need to come."

"Wolves?" Jacob asks, as he presses one hand flat on the bed to sit up.

"Yes."

Jacob nods, find his jeans on the floor, tugs them over his large bare feet. His mother steadies him as he stumbles, his foot catching in the denim trouser leg.

"Still asleep," he says, almost laughing.

Jacob zips and buttons his jeans, buckles the chafed leather belt. There's a plastic knife sheath looped on one side of his belt, but he doesn't remember where the knife is. He'll buy another from the store. He scours the floor of his room for a t-shirt as his mother leaves. She fills the kettle as he plods from his room to the kitchen, pulling a shirt over his lean stomach.

These are lean times, Camilla thinks as she brushes his cheek with her hand, kisses him before she starts breakfast. Jacob slips his bare feet inside the same boots she had worn – his boots. He dips his head to peer out of the leaded window to the right of the door, grabs a torch from the windowsill, and goes outside.

There is a tree, an oak, in the centre of the Falk family farm. Jacob swung beneath it as a child, climbed it as a teenager, he might curse it as a man, as his father does each morning, cursing it to the roots; the roots that run deep, anchoring them to the land. They will never leave. Jacob walks beneath the bough, feathers his palm over the trunk. He loves it still; he hasn't learned to hate it, not yet.

He finds his father by the ewe and turns on his torch with a click. He directs the beam at the ragged hind leg and plays it over the distended belly, encouraged by the heat of the seventh tropical night in a row in Viking lands. His father takes the torch, flicks his hand against Jacob's chest, and points to the road.

"Here comes Viktoria," his father says, as lights bump along the beech-lined gravel road running straight between the fields to the farm, three hundred metres from the Thyrup road.

"You called the vet?" Jacob points at the ewe. "It's dead."

"And so will we be if they don't listen."

"They?"

"Christiansborg. Parliament needs to listen, Jacob. We have to make them."

"But calling the vet at…" Jacob looks up at the sky. "It's not even four."

"Go and meet her."

Jacob turns, kicking at the dust as he walks across the dead grass to where Viktoria parks her car. She used to babysit when his parents went to the dance. He might have tried to kiss her once, before she married. Now he just stares when he can get away with it, shrugs when she catches him.

"A dead ewe, Jacob, what is he thinking?" she says, as she steps out of the car – a Volvo – so new the dust is streaked in apologetic lines, reluctant to cling, unlike the thick layers clogged beneath the flakes of rust on the Falk family tractor.

"He says it's wolves."

"Is that right?"

Viktoria grabs a torch from the boot of the Volvo. She clicks it on and, for just a second, the light catches her hair, teasing Jacob with a flash of lust, a memory of that *almost* kiss. Was she eight years older than him? He doesn't remember, he just watches her close the boot and then follows her as she walks along the northern wing of the farm. He jogs once to catch up until he stands beside her and his father, the three of them beside the dead sheep.

"Bo," Viktoria says, as she crouches by the sheep and examines the carcass in the light, flaring the nostrils with her fingers, lifting the hind leg with her hand. She shines the light over the ragged lacerations, nods when Bo tells Jacob to turn the sheep, and finds another wound in the belly, smears of blood caked in dust. Viktoria clicks off the torch as she stands up.

"Well?" Bo asks.

"It could be a wolf," she says. "It could be a dog."

"It's not a dog."

Viktoria sighs. "Then you don't need me, Bo. You already know what it is." She looks at him. "But what do I care? It's your money."

"Say it's a wolf."

"It might be. But we don't know."

"I saw them."

"Wolves?"

"Over there," Bo points. "Anton's seen them too."

"Anton Bjerg? He never said anything to me."

"He doesn't have sheep. The wolves are cowards, they won't touch his cattle."

"Bo," Viktoria says. "It's tourist season. You

know what it's like. The beaches are crowded, there's a dog in every other family. They get loose. Every year."

"This isn't a dog, or *dogs*, Viktoria. These are wolf bites. They are making their den, on my land."

Jacob watches his father, sees the lines crease his forehead, ticking and tugging at the skin around his eyes, as the first light fills the sky. The church spire is now visible on the low hill that presses out of the parched earth between the farm, the fields and the village. The poorer fields are yellow and dry, green only where the water is pumped and sprayed over the crops for five thousand Danish kroners a day.

A wet season, a dry season, and now wolves, denning in the woods.

"I'm calling Tilde after breakfast," Bo says.

"Tilde Sørensen?"

"From *Thyrup Dagbladet*. She'll want to talk to you."

"Why?"

"Because I'll tell her you said it was a wolf."

"For God's sake, Bo…"

Bo clenches his fists by his sides. He takes a long breath, as he waits for Viktoria to settle. Jacob lets the sheep roll back onto its side and stands up.

"Your dad had a farm, Viktoria," Bo says.

"*Had*," she says. "He went bankrupt."

"He was a friend of mine."

"Until cancer put in him a hospice." Viktoria gestures at the church. "And then Aage Dahl buried him. Right over there."

"He can see us, you know."

"It's a little early for Aage, don't you think."

"I was talking about your dad."

"I know," Viktoria says.

"Then help me," Bo says, as he reaches for Viktoria's arm. "We're struggling, this year more than most. It's the drought, and now the wolves. One takes my crops, the other my sheep. Say it's a wolf, Viktoria."

"It might be," she says, as Bo lets go of her arm.

"Say it is."

Viktoria nods, ever so quickly, and Jacob sees it. He follows her to the car when Bo tells him to. The grass, dead straw, hollow vines and husks, scratch along the leather of their shoes until they both reach the cobbles, and the dust settles between the stones. The light is stronger now, and Jacob can see strands of Viktoria's hair clinging to her cheeks, tiny beads of sweat between the top of her lip and her nose. There's not a lick of wind, nothing to hide the sudden thud and thump of teenage lust in his chest, the tingle in his fingers.

Married, he thinks.

Viktoria opens the boot of the Volvo, tosses the torch into a plastic crate, and looks at him through the glass. She almost smiles at the look in his eyes, and he wonders if she remembers the half kiss when he was seventeen.

"You've grown up," she says, as she closes the boot.

"What?" His throat is sticky, and he licks his top lip.

"Don't be like your father. He'll die on this farm, or it'll kill him, like my father."

"You said it was cancer."

"Farming is a cancer, Jacob," Viktoria says. She opens the car door and gets in. "I'll tell Tilde it's a wolf," she says.

Jacob nods, turning as his father walks past the end of the north wing, calling out something about breakfast, with a nod towards the kitchen.

"Between the bank and the politicians, what's one more predator, eh?" Viktoria says, as she starts the car.

Jacob takes a step back as she closes the door and reverses into the courtyard. He watches her go, waits until she has reached the road, and then turns to look over his shoulder at the church on the hill, and the woods below. There the wolf lurks beneath the trees, the vet will confirm it, the local paper will report it. The wolf summer begins.

Chapter 2

Jon Østergård embarrasses his daughter with a wave from the podium. The auditorium is stuffed with students chasing credits before the summer break, and professors with and without tenure, curious about the wolf in Greenland. Jon breezes through his introduction, a little too fast perhaps, as his tongue trips over the English language. But then he cycles through the first six slides of Northeast Greenland, the scene-setters and breath-takers. They never fail, and he knows he has their attention.

"It's like Alaska without trees," he says, as he clicks on to the next slide. "And here is our wolf."

Jon lingers over the image of an Arctic wolf, white fur, long, spindly legs. Its shoulders are hunched, tail slightly raised, an inch between inquisitive and afraid. Jon remembers the wolf every time he shows the slide.

"This is Gere," he says, and clicks on to the next image, "and Freke, named after Odin's wolves." Jon imagines the deep, theatrical sigh his daughter makes every time he begins the story of Odin's wolves, and how, in the barren, frozen north of Greenland, he is always reminded of the Nordic Gods. How he carries a copy of the myths on his sledge, something to read when the storms force him and his Greenlandic guide inside the canvas tent.

"Gere is three years old, mature enough to mate with Freke, although, he doesn't seem to have figured it out yet, not unlike some of you," Jon says, with a nod to the crowd. He waits for the laughter to subside, and nods at the University of Alaska Professor of biology. "It works every time, Bob," he says.

"They don't need any encouragement, Jon, believe me."

More laughs and Jon imagines Emma curling on her seat, and hiding behind her knees. This is the price of coming to Alaska – *dad jokes.*

Jon spots a hand raised by a student sitting in one of the middle rows of seats. He stands up, and Jon gestures for the students to settle to let the young man speak.

"You're not from Greenland," the student says.

"That's right. I'm Danish. But the University of Copenhagen pay me to spend my winters and the occasional summer in Greenland. It keeps me out of trouble, and out of my daughter's hair," he says, watching Emma cringe as he waves at her. He notices the heads that turn in her direction, especially the boys, and feels that strange mix of fatherly pride tempered with a sudden need to protect his nineteen-year-old daughter from the wolves.

"But aren't there wolves in Denmark?" the student asks, sitting down for Jon's reply.

"Yes, there are. They come across the border from Germany. The European wolf is similar in size to the wolves in Minnesota – anywhere from twenty to eighty kilos."

"That's about one-hundred-and-seventy-five pounds," Bob says, with a nod for Jon to continue.

"As you know, wolves have an incredible range. Denmark has a lot of deer, and perhaps it was always just a matter of time before they crossed the border. A dead wolf was discovered in one of our National Parks, in Jutland, in 2012. It died of cancer. Yes," Jon says, as he places his laser pointer on the podium, "wolves can get cancer, just like they can be infested with worms, or fleas. The popular image of the wolf is as a healthy predator, like Freke here," he gestures towards the white wolf on the screen behind him. "But wolves have a tough time of it, like all animals. Cancer took the first one in Denmark in 2012. But it was the first wolf death since 1813." Jon pauses as Bob does a quick calculation.

"One-hundred-and-ninety-nine years," he says.

"Thanks, Bob," Jon says, and waits for another roll of laughter. "I knew I could count on you."

"Anytime."

"Yes?" Jon says, as the student stands up again.

"I was wondering why…"

"Why I am studying wolves in Greenland, and not at home?"

"Yes."

"Is he on the budgetary board, Bob?" Jon says, to the delight of the students.

"No," Bob says, and stands up. He shields his eyes from the glare of the projector, and searches for the student in the crowd. "Is that you, Michael?"

"Yes, sir."

"Why am I not surprised?"

The students giggle as Bob sits down, gesturing for Jon to continue.

"It's a good question, Michael. Between you and me, I'm quite happy to do my research in Greenland." Jon pauses, as a familiar wave of peace settles over his body. It happens every time he thinks of Greenland. "I can't describe it, but maybe some of you know what it's like to be outside, far from the towns."

"We know," Bob says, as he nods to the man sitting next to him. "Some of us more than others."

Jon looks at the man, sees a little of the Greenlanders in the man's nut-brown skin, and the way he sits, as if his thoughts are collected, his body still, only his eyes are active, and they blister with a quiet energy.

"It's peaceful, undisturbed," Jon says, as he looks for the student in the middle row. "In Greenland you can get closer to the wolf, too. My daughter grows tired of me telling this story, but there was a time one spring, the sky was deep blue, but no sun. I went out of the tent to pee – a tricky task when wearing polar bear skin trousers, I can tell you." The students laugh, and Jon catches his daughter's eye. He mouths the word *sorry* and continues. "I found what I needed to find and was just getting started when something tugged at my ankle. I looked behind me and Gere had his teeth in the heel of my *kamikker* – I think you call them *mukluks*. I had to shake him off, before I could shake, if you know what I mean?"

Jon sees Emma cringe as the lecture hall fills with laughter.

"I think we know," Bob says.

"Right. Well, that's Greenland. You're closer to the wild; you live it and learn to live with it. It's not quite the same in Denmark."

"But," the student says, "that's where the problems are, aren't they?"

"Problems?"

"What Michael might be referring to is what we call *problem wolves*, the ones that take sheep, scare cattle, kill dogs. Is that right, Michael?"

"Yes, sir."

"Well, of course, that is a valid area of study," Jon says, "but my research has been wholly concentrated on wolves in Greenland. There are no settlements in the area where the wolves roam, no people, not even hunters. The Sirius Sledge Patrol has small teams patrolling a vast area – just two men and eleven dogs per team – and then there's me and my guide, maybe the occasional expedition." Jon shrugs. "No problem wolves, just plenty of problems – the usual in the Arctic."

"Wouldn't you like to study wolves in Denmark?" the student asks.

"Ah, well," Jon says, "perhaps that's a question for my daughter." He points to where she sits, and the students turn their heads once more. "What do you think, Emma?"

Emma uncurls her knees and crosses her arms across her chest. "Would you be living at home, in Copenhagen?"

"The wolves are in Jutland. I would be away a lot."

"Then I guess that's fine," she says, and the students laugh. "So long as you're away, a lot."

"It seems," Jon says, "that I am the *problem*, not the wolves." He chuckles and points at the slide. "Let me tell you more about Gere and Freke, and then I can take more questions."

The students wait until Jon's last slide, saving their questions until the end of the lecture, and when Bob senses they are getting restless. He sends them away to their next class, waits for Emma to join them on the stage, and then introduces Jon to the man who had been sitting beside him during Jon's presentation.

"Jon, I'd like you to meet David McGrath. He's our local expert."

"Local?" David says.

"You're local, now you're living in Fairbanks," Bob says, with a wink. "I'll leave you to get acquainted. I have a class." He shakes Jon's hand. "We'll talk before your flight."

"Thanks, Bob."

"Our pleasure."

Bob smiles at Emma and then leaves.

"Coffee?" David says, and waits for Jon to stuff his computer into his satchel.

He leads them out of the auditorium and along the hall to the canteen area. The students fill the room with chatter that rises and twists between the rafters in the ceiling until class starts and the canteen empties. Emma blushes as Jon nods at a group of boys and says something to her in Danish.

"I have a daughter your age," David says, as he places a tray of coffee and a bottle of coke on their table. "Her name is Nukilik."

"What does it mean?" Emma asks.

"It means she is strong," David says, as he empties the tray and places it on the floor between the chair legs. "Have you met many Eskimo in Greenland, Jon?"

"I think they like to be called Greenlanders, but I don't see many people when I am in the field."

"Before I became a *local*," David says, "I lived in Barrow. That's on the coast. It's the northernmost city in Alaska. I am Iñupiat, Eskimo."

"And you have wolves up there?"

"Some. Maybe. I study wolves here, in Fairbanks."

"Problem wolves?"

"The wolves don't think so."

David sips his coffee and smiles at Emma. The

mid-morning sun streams in through the canteen windows and Emma squints as she opens her cola. The light catches the freckles on her pale skin, and she notices David staring at her. She withers, and he smiles again.

"Forgive me," he says. "There are many white Alaskans, but I am still surprised when I see Scandinavian blue eyes. So young."

"Young?" Jon asks.

"Young in the ways of the wolf. The Danish people will remember the wolf as it was described in the Middle Ages, the coward, the devil, a personification of the evil nature of man. Something to be punished, tortured, as if by punishing the wolf they exorcised their evil ways, the crueller the better."

"I don't know, David," Jon says. He takes Emma's hand as the man's strange words lean towards a rant, rather than a scientific observation.

"You'll see," he says. "If you want to."

"What I want is to study the wolf. I can do that in Greenland, or in Denmark, if that's what I'm told to do." The light tone of the presentation seems far away as Jon feels a weight press down upon his shoulders. Wolf-weight, about eighty kilos, one-hundred-and-seventy pounds, enough to curl his shoulders towards the table.

"It will be difficult," David says. "Biologists, like you, look for facts. The wolf is measured in a scientific context. It is observed. I'm telling you this because I have seen it. The biologists I know cannot see the wolf for the science. They put a radio collar around its neck to find out where it is, where it has been, they do not bother to look where it is going." David pulls a business card from his pocket. "I enjoyed your presentation," he says. "If you think I can help, then you can reach me on this number." He stands up. "Remember to look where it is going, look beyond and ahead of the wolf if you want to get to know it."

David shakes Jon's hand. He dips his head at Emma, carries his coffee mug out of the canteen. He doesn't look back.

"That was odd," Jon says.

"What did he mean about the Middle Ages, dad? It's 2018."

"I suppose he means that people's views haven't changed."

"In two hundred years?"

"I know. I don't believe it either."

Emma looks at the entrance to the canteen. She pictures the Eskimo standing there and notices his image on the poster for the Museum of the North in Fairbanks, just across the parking lot. She wonders who he really is, wonders about his people.

"He was a little weird, dad," she says.

"He was, but…"

"But what?"

"I don't know. I guess it's just as well I study Arctic wolves."

"But would you study wolves at home, in Denmark?"

"Would you want me to?"

"Maybe," Emma says. "Next year is my last year of Gymnasium. It would be nice to have you at home. At least for a little while."

"Really?"

"Sure, as long as you don't embarrass me."

"Ah, Emma," Jon says. "I think we both know

that's impossible."

Chapter 3

The wolves are at the door, thinks Felix Poulsen, Danish Minister for Environment and Food. He sits in his office, flicking through the latest in a series of articles about so-called problem wolves, this time from a local paper in Thyrup. He buzzes for his secretary.

"Where the hell is Thyrup?" he asks, as his secretary walks into his office.

"West Jutland," he says, "about two kilometres from the sea. It's a little north of Ringkøbing."

"And the journalist?" Felix says, with a glance at the article, "Tilde Sørensen?"

"Local. Competent. Fairly aggressive."

"Hungry?"

"Very. Like most of the young journalists on the west coast, she wants to write for *JydskeVestkysten*."

"I think she already does. They seem to have paraphrased her article with an online version already."

"She has the voice of the people."

Felix laughs. "Such a cliché."

"Yes."

"And my two o'clock?"

"Is Lærke Wang from *Danmarks Radio*."

"Television?"

"Yes. Live, I'm afraid."

"And they want a comment on problem wolves." Felix shuffles the article into a folder and nods for his secretary to leave. "Wait, one more thing. I asked you to find me an expert."

"Yes," the secretary checks the notepad app in his phone. "His name is Jon Østergård. He's flying in from Alaska today. I can have someone meet him at the airport."

"Do that," Felix says, and stands up. He looks at his watch. "What time does he get in?"

"Four o'clock. I got the flight number from the University. He will be tired."

"I'm sure he will. I'll meet with him at five." Felix walks to the door. "And where do I have to do the interview?"

"On the front steps."

Felix straightens his tie as he walks down the stairs to the main entrance of Christiansborg, the parliament building for the Danish *Folketing*. He finds the building less impressive today than he did a year ago, when he accepted the ministerial post from his party leader. Coalition or not, *Venstre* was still the ruling party, *his* party. He suppresses the usual thoughts of party leadership that often trip him up at inopportune moments, and concentrates on his appearance first, comments second. He knows Lærke will lead with the drought, the wolf is a secondary matter, lost in the heat of the summer, or so he hopes.

Lærke is not alone when he finds her outside the building. Felix ignores the small crowd of tourists bustling beside the television van, with the large red letters DR blazed across the white panels. The van is topped with an aerial dish and there's a camera crew waiting beside the van next to Lærke. She nods for Felix to stand in front of the building, and smiles as an assistant mops her brow. A thermometer might read twenty-eight degrees, but Felix thinks it is over thirty.

That's her lead, he reminds himself, *the weather, and the drought*, then *the wolves*.

"Minister Poulsen," she says, a second after the crew signal that they are ready. "Farmers are spending five-thousand kroner a day to water their fields. How does the government intend to compensate them?"

"As you know, we are working closely with the European Commissioner for Agriculture to support farmers in Denmark. Funding is available for farmers in the EU suffering from the drought, and Danish farmers have not been forgotten. These are exceptional times, as you are aware, and every effort is being made to accommodate the difficulties farmers are facing during this difficult time."

"And yet, twenty farms declared bankruptcy in June, with more on the way. Isn't this a case of too little too late?"

"I think you'll find that the Commission is monitoring the drought situation very closely, as demonstrated by advance payments of up to seventy five percent, and the lifting of diversification requisites under these exceptional circumstances."

"By exceptional circumstances, Minister, do you mean the temperature?"

"And the lack of rain, yes. While tourists might enjoy the heat, we know that farmers are suffering. We are working hand in hand with the Commission to address the adverse weather conditions."

"The exceptional circumstances."

"Yes," Felix says. He tries to hide the frown of anticipation as he wonders what tack she will take next. And then he realises, they are finished discussing the drought.

"Would you not say that the growing wolf population in Denmark affecting farmers on the west coast also falls under the category of exceptional circumstances?"

"You're going to have to be more specific, Lærke."

"How about the problem wolves attacking livestock on farms, farms that are already suffering from poor crops. What is the government doing to address *that* problem?"

"Wolves are, as you know, protected by European Law."

"But they are killing sheep and cattle."

"Allegedly," Felix says. "We still need documented proof."

"And a veterinarian's examination is not good enough?"

"You're referring to the Thyrup wolf?"

"Wolves. There is a den in the area."

"We are addressing the problem," Felix says, and bites back a curse as he realises what he has said.

"So, you agree that they are a problem?"

"Denmark is not the only European country to have wolves, Lærke. I am in regular communication with my colleagues in France and Germany, about this very matter."

"Problem wolves?"

"Wolves in general."

"And how is it that the EU is willing to pour millions into agricultural relief, and yet has nothing to offer the farmers losing livestock to large predators crossing borders?"

"The government considers each case individually. If there is just cause for compensation, farmers will be compensated."

"But you're not going to allow them to protect their livelihood?"

"I don't follow?"

"You're not going to allow them to shoot the wolves?"

Felix pauses, conscious of the camera focusing on his face.

"The wolf is protected by European law," he says. "Thank you."

Lærke lowers her microphone as the crew begins to pack their gear. She catches Felix by the arm and walks with him towards the main entrance.

"I'm going to Thyrup," she says.

"I'm sure you are."

"Why don't you come with me?"

Felix stops and loosens his tie. "Are you punting for a job in media relations? I thought you preferred life in front of the camera?"

"I'm just saying it would make a good story."

"You have a good *story*."

"You don't think it's true, do you?"

Felix smiles as he reaches for the door. "Have a nice day, Lærke."

It is cooler inside. The thick concrete and granite-covered facades beat back the heat, as Felix walks up the stairs to his office. Lærke's suggestion to visit Thyrup rattles around his mind as he pauses at his secretary's desk to check for missed calls. His secretary hands him a handwritten message – a comment from the Prime Minister's office about the interview. He returns to his office and waits while his secretary puts him through and the Prime Minister answers his call.

Micro-*managing*, Felix thinks, as the Prime Minister praises him for the comments about the drought, and then roasts him for his handling of the wolf.

"What else could I say?" he says.

"You could have given them a name."

"Whose?"

"The expert you have assigned to the committee investigating the wolf."

"I don't have one yet," Felix says. "An expert, I mean."

"Why the hell not?"

"He's arriving later today."

"And his name?"

"Jon Østergård. The University assures me he is their best researcher when it comes to the wolf," Felix says, as he clicks on the information packet his secretary prepared earlier. Images of Greenland fill the screen and a man with frosted eyebrows and ice clinging to his beard grins back at Felix. There is a white wolf in the background, and Felix clicks the screen to enlarge it.

"Don't make me get involved, Felix," the Prime Minister says, and hangs up.

Felix replaces the phone in its cradle, and clicks through a resume of Østergård's experience, including three winter research expeditions over the last four years, and a summer trip to Ellesmere Island in Canada. Østergård was married, now divorced, and has a nineteen-year-old daughter. He lives in Copenhagen, but is used to travelling.

Felix buzzes for his secretary. "Anything more on Østergård?"

"Like what?" his secretary says, as he hovers at the door.

"Anything the press could use if they wanted to discredit him."

"That's his career." The secretary points at the computer screen.

"And his divorce?"

"Nothing out of the ordinary. His ex-wife lives in Spain."

"And what does she do?"

"I believe she works for the Ministry of Agriculture, Fisheries and Food."

"Huh," Felix says. He stares at his secretary, slightly concerned that he overlooked or downgraded such a significant piece of information. "And you didn't think that was important?"

"She's not available."

"I don't understand."

"She also studies wolves, in Spain."

"So, she's the Spanish equivalent of her ex-husband?"

"In a manner of speaking."

"Find me her number," Felix says, as he opens a search engine in his browser He reads about the Iberian wolf, a subspecies of the grey wolf, *Canis lupus*. It is the grey wolf that people say they have seen in Denmark. Felix clicks further and learns that there are roughly two-thousand wolves roaming Spain and Portugal, a far cry from the handful reported in Denmark. While Spain is a popular holiday destination for Danes, it seems that the wolf outside their door at home is a lot more frightening than the wolf outside the caravan door during the holidays. Felix closes the browser and turns on the television to catch the news and the rerun of his interview just an hour earlier.

Lærke Wang, it seems, has chosen this story to be her big break, framing the interview with emotionally-charged words, evoking scenes of suffering, where desperate farming communities feel isolated, ignored by the government, and threatened by roving predators. Felix wonders when Lærke decided to drop DR's responsibility to remain objective, and then he sees why, as the local camera crew follow a farmer through a parched paddock to disturbing images of the bloated carcass of a sheep. Lærke's voice cuts in as the camera follows the farmer to a temporary fence, explaining it is a fence that the farmer cannot afford but needs to build to save what he can of his flock.

"And he's not alone," she says. "There are many stories like this one. Here, at the Falk family farm, generations have farmed the West Jutland fields, all the way back to the 1800s, when it was legal and expected for a farmer to protect his land by all means possible, long before the rise of the European Union, and laws that make it illegal for a farmer to kill a wolf."

Felix mutes the wall-mounted television and tosses the remote onto his desk. He picks up the phone on the first ring, writes a number on the pad beside the computer, and then dials the number of an office in the Ministry building in Madrid. He speaks English when they answer, and wonders if he has been understood, as the phone clicks for a few moments until a static hush clouds the line.

"Hello?" Felix says.

He hears a muted conversation, and then a woman's voice, clearer now, as if the phone was pressed against her clothes, and now she is ready to speak.

"Elin Møller."

"Not Østergård?"

"That was my husband's name. Who is this?"

Felix switches to Danish, and says, "My name is Felix Poulsen. I'm the Danish Minister for Environment and Food; I'd like to talk to you about your husband, and about wolves, if you have the time."

"Is Jon in trouble?"

"No, not at all," Felix says. "Why would you say that?"

"I've seen the news," she says. "You think you have a wolf problem."

"Well, some people do."

"And you've hired Jon to look into it?"

"His name has come up, yes."

Felix frowns at the sound of the static on the line. This time, there is no muted discussion, and he wonders if Elin Møller is taking a moment to think, and why.

"I've got ten minutes," she says.

Chapter 4

Thyrup church has a commanding view of the village, the surrounding fields and farms, birds and beasts. Little is missed, few things are overlooked, and nothing is forgotten. The church building is white, with three tiered roofs, from the bell tower, the main hall, and the entrance. The roof of Thyrup church is clay-red, and each roof is separated with a crenulated division of white stone. The building is sturdy and has weathered many seasons, just like its Lutheran Priest, Aage Dahl. Like the church building, his reach is wide and lengthy, his observation obscured only on cloudy days. On such days he relies on his congregation to keep him informed of the ins and outs and comings and goings of his flock. In a farming community such as Thyrup, the shepherd and flock metaphor is particularly apt. As is the story of the wolf, something he reminds his congregation about whenever possible.

The wolf is the Devil's dog let loose on the earth, he thinks, and with good reason. Why shouldn't the wolf roam among the sinners of West Jutland? What better way to root out evil than to follow the wolf, to see where it has been, and to lend a hand, a supportive ear, and a friendly word to those about to stray from the true path.

These are his thoughts as he bumps along the gravel between the beech trees to the Falk family farm. The local television crew is just leaving as he parks his car beside Bo's tractor. Aage sees Bo talking with his son as he gets out of his car. He stretches and then lights a cigarette, resting on the bonnet as Bo walks over to him.

"Hello, Jacob," Aage says and waves, as the

young man tries to skirt around the building. He will talk to him later, once Bo invites him inside for coffee and a bowl of Camilla's homemade buttermilk and sweet biscuits.

"Don't mind him," Bo says, as he shakes Aage's hand. "He's got a lot on his mind."

"I don't see him in church very often."

"He'll be there on Sunday."

"I don't have to tell you how important it is," Aage says. "Regular attendance, that's the answer. It's such a shame that the young and their parents have turned their back on the church. There are more Germans than Danes at my service these days."

"Tourists?"

"Yes." Aage finishes his cigarette, pinches the tip and slips it into the packet. "But that's not why I'm here."

"You heard about the wolf?"

"I heard about an attack. I *read* about a wolf. Tilde is a very passionate writer, wouldn't you agree, Bo?"

"She listens well."

"She does. Let's walk," Aage says, and points to the paddock behind the farm. He is quiet until they reach the dead sheep. "Are you just going to let it rot?"

"I can't eat it or sell it; I may as well milk it."

"For all it's worth?"

"What's that supposed to mean?"

"It's thirty degrees, Bo, and not a breath of wind. It has served its purpose. Bury it."

"If it's buried, it can't be seen."

Aage gestures at the fence. "You put that up today?"

"We started at first light."

Aage walks to the fence, places his hand on top of the chicken wire and shrugs. "It's not very sturdy, nor is it very high."

"It is what it is."

"Like the sheep," Aage says.

"I think you're trying to tell me something."

Aage looks at the church, blistering white on the hilltop like a beacon. *It misses nothing*, he thinks, and gestures for Bo to follow him. They walk the length of the fence, past the stile and on to a copse of trees that provides a whisper of shade, from which they cannot see the church.

"If the sheep is seen it can be studied. Bury it, Bo, before someone finds a dog hair, or something else to suggest it is not the wolf that is to blame, merely the fear of the wolf itself."

"I'm not afraid of wolves."

"Maybe not, but you resent it, don't you?"

Bo stares at Aage as he lights another cigarette.

"It must be the heat. Your riddles are more complicated than usual."

"It's not a riddle," Aage says, "It's a fact. The wolf is a free agent. It roams where it wants, takes what it wants. It pays no taxes, it has no debts. It is rootless, and its future is open, it is free, and yet it sucks from the working man's teats. It drains him. I would hate it too, if I were a farmer."

Bo reaches for Aage's cigarette and takes a drag. He blows the smoke up through the leaves of the lower branches before he hands it back. Aage watches him. He sees the worry and worse, he sees a broken man who thinks no further than half a year at a time, as if the farm might close before the next harvest. If

Aage asks him, Bo will probably tell him he hopes it is this harvest, not the next. He doesn't think he can survive another. Perhaps the only thing that keeps Bo alive, perhaps the only way to save the man, to save his family, and the farm, is to give him an outlet, to give him something to hate.

"There is a meeting at the village hall on Wednesday," Aage says. "Will you come?"

"Is it about the wolf?"

"Yes. You've seen the groups on Facebook?"

"Hah, ask Jacob," Bo says. "I don't have time for that."

"They are very proactive. You might find friends there."

"I have friends."

Aage nods. "Different friends, then." He finishes his cigarette and wipes his brow.

"Do you want to come in?" Bo asks.

"For a bowl of Camilla's buttermilk?"

"If Jacob hasn't eaten it all."

Aage laughs and follows Bo to the farmhouse. The leaves on the oak's lower branches are yellowing in the heat, and the cobbles are littered with leaf fall. *It is not yet August,* Aage thinks, as he kicks the dust from his shoes and follows Bo inside.

Camilla keeps a tidy kitchen, it is the hub of the farm. The flagstones are swept, the table wiped, and the filter coffee fresh. She greets Aage with a hug, kisses her husband, and calls for Jacob to join them.

"Strawberry buttermilk?" Aage asks.

"Two good things about the summer," she says, as she sets the table. "Strawberries and butterflies."

Jacob joins them, sliding onto the bench along the wall by the window. He nods when Aage catches his eye.

"How has your summer been, Jacob?" he asks.

"It's okay."

"You're finished with Gymnasium?"

"He's got one more year," Camilla says. "Jacob starts 3G in August."

"Good, good," Aage says. He thanks Camilla for his coffee and takes a portion of buttermilk when she slips a ladle into the bowl.

"Did you see the television crew?" she asks.

"They were just leaving." Aage slides the bowl across the table towards Jacob. "I didn't talk to them."

"But you read Tilde's article."

"Yes."

"And what do you think?"

Camilla waits, leaning against her husband as Aage finishes his first spoonful of buttermilk.

"It's very good," he says. And, when Camilla frowns, "I liked the article too."

"Oh," she says, and laughs.

Jacob fills his bowl to the brim, slopping thick buttermilk over the sides, as he drops a handful of round sweet biscuits onto the strawberry surface. Camilla throws a wet cloth at him and it slips off his shoulder and onto the table. Bo sips his coffee without a word.

Aage smiles as Camilla sits next to him. He takes a handful of biscuits and places them beside his bowl. "A few years ago, studded collars were all the rage," he says. "You know the ones I mean, Jacob? Girls wore them mostly and I often wondered why. There were metal spikes on their collars, the straps of their bags, their shoes. The spikes were rounded, but some were quite long. I often wondered if they could fly with them, on planes," he says, and pauses as Camilla humours him with a smile. "Do you know where they came from?"

"The collars?"

"They used to put wolf collars around the necks of dogs protecting livestock. The Spanish call the collars *carlancas*. The spikes on them were long, made of iron," Aage says, and straightens his finger. "Wolves go for the neck, clamping, gripping, and suffocating their prey, while another goes for the belly. They've been known to eat a deer before it is dead." He nods as Jacob looks up. "Sometimes they lie beside the animal, panting, waiting for it to die before they eat it, depending on how tired they are, after the hunt. Sometimes they leave it, without as much as a nibble."

"They kill it and don't eat it?" Jacob asks.

"For fun." Aage picks up one of the biscuits and drops it into the buttermilk.

Bo reaches for the ladle and fills half his bowl. He adds the biscuits, tapping them with the spoon as the priest speaks.

"These girls, the ones with the collars, they couldn't know they were wearing wolf collars, and neither could they know that just a few hundred years ago, those collars might have come in handy, to protect them from werewolves." Aage smiles, as Jacob stops eating.

"He's joking," Camilla says, and wipes the buttermilk from the table around Jacob's bowl.

"I wish I was," Aage says. "But that's what people believed, and they treated men and women harshly if they thought they were werewolves, or perhaps they had slept with one. People were burned at the stake, burned alive." Aage winks at Jacob, and smiles when the young man grins back at him.

"There are no werewolves in Denmark," Bo says. "Just real ones."

"Which brings me back to the collar," Aage says. "Have you thought about getting a dog, to protect the flock?"

"A sheep dog?" Bo frowns.

"I was thinking of something a little bigger."

"Something you put a collar on," Jacob says.

"Perhaps."

"Dogs cost money," Bo says. "And they need feeding. Fences don't."

"There's more than one way a dog can help you, Bo," Aage says.

Bo sighs. "And you know where I might find one?"

"There's a German Shepherd at the dog home in Ringkøbing. I found it online." Aage reaches into his shirt pocket and pulls out a folded piece of paper. "It's a few years old," he says, as he slides the paper across the table to Bo. "It's a little aggressive, and the family couldn't cope. A good dog, by all accounts. Perfect for the farm, I think."

"I've always wanted a dog," Jacob says. "I'm fed up with cats."

"You'll be the one to look after it then."

"Actually, Bo, I think it would be best if it was you who looked after it." Aage shrugs at Jacob. "Your father needs a hobby," he says, smiling. Aage thanks Camilla for the buttermilk, the coffee, and the company, and nods towards to the oak. "I'll have a smoke before I head back to the church," he says.

"Will you join me, Bo?"

"Jacob will clear the table," Camilla says. She ruffles his hair as he protests.

Once outside, Aage lights a cigarette and offers the packet to Bo. They smoke for a few minutes without talking; listening for the wind they can see tickling the very tops of the trees near the church.

"Bury the sheep, Bo," Aage says. "Before someone looks at it."

"You don't think it was a wolf?"

"It doesn't matter. Just get rid of it. And get that dog," he says. "I think you'll find it useful."

"For guarding my sheep? What if it eats them? What then?"

"You're a clever man, Bo. You have a beautiful wife, a strong son, and a farm with deep roots. I hate to see a man like you get dragged down. Bury the sheep, buy the dog, come to the meeting. We'll talk then."

"The meeting is Wednesday?"

"That's right," Aage says, as he walks across the cobbles to his car. "And I expect to see you on Sunday. Tell Jacob I'll be talking about werewolves."

Chapter 5

Jon sleeps on the flight from Anchorage to London, while Emma works her way through a whole series of *Friends*, waking her dad as they arrive at Heathrow, and then yawning her way through security and onto the flight home to Copenhagen. It's her turn to sleep as Jon refuels with coffee and a newspaper. The drought dominates the first few pages, together with fires in Sweden, the football World Cup, and an article squeezed between farming subsidies and heat wave stories. The paper flaps, knocking Emma's hand, as Jon folds it to read the article. It seems that any headline about a wolf attack continues to draw the crowds, and the leader below the picture of the bloated body of a dead sheep suggests such attacks might increase as a denning pair have been spotted in West Jutland. The article goes on to say that if the litter survives, it will be the first pack of wolves to be raised in Denmark as far as anyone knows. Jon finds more opinions in the column reserved for readers' letters. They might be balanced in number, but each opinion is biased – for and against. Only the wolf's opinion is missing – no-one speaks for the wolf, only about it. Emma stirs as Jon folds and creases the newspaper into a manageable size, swatting his daughter on the thigh as she wakes.

"We're landing soon," he says.

"Nearly home," she says, and closes her eyes.

"Emma."

"Huh."

"You're snoring again."

"I don't snore, dad," she says, and then the captain orders the flight attendants to prepare for landing and they see the pale runway shimmering in the heat below.

The land around it is parched – scorched earth, with tiny pockets of green, revealing a water wealth not shared by the rest of the country. Jon recalls the articles about the drought, imagines how the farmers might be suffering, and then realises he has no idea. There are no farmers in his family, not that he remembers. Ironic, he thinks, when Østergård could be translated as *eastern farm*. He smiles at the thought as they land, and then the air-conditioning is switched off, and all he thinks about is the heat.

"Next time we go to Alaska, can we actually *see* Alaska?" Emma says, as Jon places their luggage on a trolley. "Not just one town for four days."

"You want to go back?"

"Sure, it was fun."

"Even when I teased you?" Jon says, as he pushes the trolley to the exit.

"You've been teasing me my whole life, but this time you did it in English, and your English sucks, dad."

"You don't think I can speak English?"

"You can speak it, but your accent… urgh."

"*Urgh*? That's enlightening. How about some examples? Like when I say…" Jon stops as they pass through the door and into arrivals. He sees a sign with his name printed in thick black letters.

"Who's that, dad?"

"I don't know." He pushes the trolley towards the man holding the sign.

"Jon Østergård?"

"Yes."

"The Minister for Environment and Food sent

me. I'm to take you to Christiansborg. He hopes you have time to meet him?"

"Urgh," Emma says, and leans against her father.

"It'll just be an hour, and then I will drive you home."

"What's it about?"

"I'm just the driver," the man says, as he takes their bags from the trolley. "This way."

"A whole hour," Emma says, as she follows her dad. "I just want to go home…"

"You're whining."

"I'm tired."

"But not curious? You did hear that we're going to Christiansborg? That's the parliament, Folketing."

"I know where and what it is, dad. Mum works for the same ministry, remember?"

"In Spain," Jon says, as he works hard not to picture his ex-wife every time he looks at his daughter. Emma is the spitting image.

"Spain, *same*, dad. All boring."

"You can take the metro," he says, fishing the keys to the apartment from his pocket.

"It's too hot," she says, and then points at the man putting their bags into the boot of a black BMW. "Air-conditioning," she says, and runs to the car. The man opens the door, and she slides onto the back seat.

Emma laps up the cool air in the back of the car as the Friday afternoon traffic slows them down. The driver apologises, Jon says it can't be helped, flicking his head towards the back seat at each *beep* and *burr* of Emma's smartphone.

"There was no Internet on the flight," he says, as if the driver requires an explanation.

"I have kids," the man says, "and a wife. She's worse than them."

Jon laughs, and Emma's phone continues to beep with notifications all the way to Christiansborg. The driver parks and Jon teases Emma out of the back seat and all the way into the parliament building. They pass through security, and then follow the driver up the stairs to where Felix Poulsen's secretary greets them and leads them to a meeting room. Emma finds a chair at the back of the room, uncoils her headphones and slips them over her ears, while Jon waits. His secretary promises he won't have to wait for long and just a few moments later, Felix enters the room.

"Jon Østergård," he says, and shakes Jon's hand. "Thank you for coming."

"It must be urgent," Jon says, as Felix pours him a cup of coffee.

"Urgent? Yes, I suppose it is." He gestures for them to sit at the table. "Your daughter?"

"When she's on this planet," Jon says. "How can I help you?"

"I've been looking through your file, done some background reading, talked with your colleagues... I even talked with your ex-wife."

"Why would you do that?"

"Background. I need to know who you are."

"But, my wife..."

"Said some very nice things about you. I'm not sure there are many ex-wives out there who would do the same."

"I've only got the one."

"Yes," Felix says. "Of course."

Jon takes a sip of coffee and looks around the

room. The mahogany panels are as thick as church pews, the table thicker. The light bulbs are new – reactive to the light. It's warm inside the room, and Jon takes a napkin to wipe his brow.

"It's worse if I open the window," Felix says.

"It's alright." Jon stuffs the napkin into his pocket. "You want to know about wolves?"

"That's right. You've been keeping up to date on the wolf situation in Denmark?"

"I thought we only had a handful of wolves. That's not quite a situation."

"The public would disagree."

Jon nods as he thinks back to David McGrath's strange comments in the canteen in Fairbanks. Something about looking where the wolf was going, not where it had been.

"Those reports in the newspaper," Jon says. "The attacks? They were probably dogs."

"I don't disagree, but neither can I make such a statement. Not without proof."

"Then have the carcass examined by a vet."

"Vets don't have experience with wolves, Jon. Not much anyway." Felix refills their cups with coffee; the steam from the thermal jug hangs just above the lid. "I need someone to assess the situation, get a feel for the mood, cut through the hysteria and make a determination based on fact, details, and their own experience from the field."

"What kind of determination?"

"With your proposal a White Paper could be drawn up, explaining what the government might do to address the problem wolves that are splitting the nation."

"Problem wolves?"

"Yes, the ones attacking sheep, scaring families, and generally disturbing the status quo."

"You mean the *human* status quo."

Felix nods. "When it comes to fear, we're a primitive, instinctual race, Jon. But fear can be a powerful wedge that can split a country." Felix points towards Emma. "I'm sure your daughter can tell you just how nasty people can be online. I think the word is *toxic*."

"I'm on Facebook," Jon says, "but I tend to avoid posting or reading comments. I think they call them trolls – the *nasty people*."

"This isn't *trolling*, Jon. We're talking about communities of people split by differences of opinion. And it's not just about facts versus fiction. This is deep-rooted. Many people hate wolves, and I mean truly hate. I've seen forums where people discuss the best way to inflict pain on a wolf. Not just kill it, but to cause it real pain. These people have been applauded."

"The wolf has a chequered past," Jon says. "It's true. But I'm not sure I'm the best person for the job."

"Why not?" Felix says, and frowns. He gestures at a folder on the table. "Your experience suggests otherwise."

"My experience is with wolves, Minister. You're asking me to study people."

"No, I'm asking you to study problem wolves, to find out if there is a problem."

"Involving people," Jon says. He stifles a yawn. "Sorry, it's been a long flight."

"Perhaps you need time to think about it. But really, Jon, this is a perfect opportunity for you to study wolves at home in Denmark."

"And their relation to people. I'm a biologist, not a psychologist. I know how wolves behave. I can't begin to tell you how people behave."

Felix takes out his phone as it beeps. He places it on the table. "Just think about it – two species – human and wolf. Humans can use one of these," he says, and swipes his thumb across his phone. "We also have the intelligence to imagine and build one. We can put a man, a woman, even monkeys into space. Such heights we can aspire to. Such energy we can apply and yet a simple animal can reduce us to a paralytic fear, rendering us incapable of rational thought. Try telling wolf-haters that there hasn't been a single case of wolves attacking people in Europe for fifty years and they turn to Wikipedia, and produce reams of attacks, mostly in Iran or Russia, anywhere but Denmark. Tell the same people that one-hundred-and-eighty-three people were killed on Danish roads in 2017, or that road injury is one of the top ten causes of death according to the World Health Organization, and they will change the subject or say it's not relevant. It's like questioning Christians about God." Felix lifts his hands in apology. "Sorry. It's the heat. It's been a long day."

"I understand," Jon says. "People don't need a reason to hate the wolf."

"No."

"And they won't listen to facts, statistics. None of these things will change their position."

"They won't."

"Then why send me to study problem wolves in Denmark?"

"Because," Felix says, with another sigh, "If I'm

going to allow them to be shot, I need a reason."

"The wolf is protected by European Law."

"I know. Your wife told me the same thing. She also wondered why Denmark should be any different from other countries. As if we could interpret the rules. People are living with wolves all over Europe."

Jon smiles. He allows himself to picture his ex-wife, hear her voice, and remember how it felt to lose an argument. She has the facts, and she always wins.

"It's like the border situation, isn't it? Policing our borders to keep migrants out."

"If only it was that simple," Felix says, and then, "I shouldn't have said that."

"It's okay, I understand."

"Then you'll help me?"

Jon looks at Emma, smiles as her hair curls and lifts as she moves her head to the rhythm of the latest track on her Spotify playlist. She has three weeks before the start of her third and final year in Gymnasium. She needs to continue at that school, and they can't commute from West Jutland. But three weeks? *It's possible*, he thinks, at least to get a feel for the situation, a chance to speak for the wolf.

"Emma starts school in the second week of August."

"But you would be willing to go there now?"

"Where is *there* exactly?"

"Thyrup," Felix says. "It's a small village close to the sea. There's a nature commission house in the area. It's yours until the end of the summer."

"Alright," Jon says. "We'd better go home and pack."

Chapter 6

Emma is silent from Copenhagen to Korsør. The water of the Great Belt between Zealand and Funen glistens as they pass through the toll and drive over the bridge. There is a lighthouse on the left before the island of Funen; it's where they sent crazy women. *I'd rather be there*, she thinks, *anywhere but Jutland.* Her father is robbing her of the last three weeks of her holiday. She wants to be with her friends. She needs her friends.

They cross the bridge and see signs for Odense. Jon talks about the beach, about how he took her there as a child and they haven't been there since.

"No wonder," she says. "It's just a beach, and crappy shops, like a mall spread across the road, with shitty things to buy, and amber bracelets, amber earrings, amber *everything.*"

"Emma."

"No, dad, you're ruining my holiday."

"I took you to Alaska."

"For *four* days. No-one goes to Alaska for four days, dad. No-one."

Jon puts the car in cruise control and they don't talk until the exit ramp before Odense, the one with the McDonald's.

"I need a coffee," Jon says, and drives off the motorway.

He parks and removes the key from the ignition with a sigh. Emma checks her messages, and then records and sends a moody *snap* to her friends.

"How long are we going to sit here, dad? It's hot."

"There's air-conditioning inside."

"I'm a vegetarian."

"Fries are vegetarian," he says and opens the door.

The heat shimmers between the cars in the parking lot, the traffic on the motorway stirs the air like a cheap fan, and Jon starts to sweat. Emma gets out of the car, shuts the door and crosses the parking area, her head down, her mind absorbed and her mood suitably pissed-off. A car pulls away from the drive-thru window right in front of Emma, who is oblivious. Jon shouts and his daughter stops, inches from impact, and the driver shakes his head.

"Come on," Jon says, tempted to take his daughter's elbow, to steer her to the door.

Emma finds a table and Jon orders. She is still embedded in her apps and streams of gossipy updates when he sits beside her, places an order of fries and a milkshake in front of her – Emma's usual order.

"It's only for a few weeks," he says, and unwraps his burger.

"You could have said no."

"I was asked by the government to do a job, Emma. You don't say *no* to that."

"That's what mum always says," she says, and slaps her phone on the table. "The government is no big deal, dad. You and mum always think they are so important, but in fact they're just boring, doing boring things."

"You sound like a teenager."

"I *am* a teenager," she says, and lifts her chin.

"Thirteen, I meant."

He regrets it as soon as he says it. Emma reaches for her phone, stops, and holds her head in such a way that Jon almost looks around to see who might be listening, who might observe the onslaught he is about to receive, probably deserves, but would prefer to be private.

"You want adult talk?"

"What?"

"You want me to talk like an adult, so that you can understand. Is that right?"

"Emma…" he says and reaches for her hand.

"Passion and drive," she says. "That's what the government is missing. They're obsessed with image, message and spin. When something happens, there's always a politician ready to speak out and demand something be done, some law to be changed, just because they want to be seen to understand the people. You know, the ones who vote for them. But they didn't have that thought a month before, not even the night before. They react, all the time. They don't think ahead, they don't…"

Look where the wolf is going, Jon thinks, *only where it's been.*

"… and then they change what they say when something else happens, or they realise that it didn't work, or it wasn't popular. Mum moved to Spain, but it's no different. It doesn't mean anything when the government asks you to do something, dad."

"Who then?" he asks.

"What?"

"If someone or some group asked you to do something, who should it be? Who would you say *yes* to?"

Jon eats while Emma thinks. She glances at her phone, as Jon adds milk to his coffee.

"Someone like Google," she says. "They change things. They don't react, they *proact*."

"I'm sure they have to react too, Emma."

"Sure, if they have to fix something. But they are always working on something. Something new, different."

"Not boring."

"That's right," she says. She smiles, just for a second.

"So, if Google asked you to do something, you'd say *yes*."

"I would." Emma sips her milkshake, cultivating the thoughtful fold of skin on her brow. "Not to just anything, it would have to mean something."

"The reason we are here – it means something, Emma, to a lot of people."

"Weirdos in deepest, darkest, Jutland."

"That's not fair."

"No? You've heard what they say about us *Københavnere*. They think we're arrogant and *distanced* just because we live in the capital of Denmark, like that's our fault."

"And they're stupid because they live in the country?"

"Yes," she says. "Of course, they are."

Jon almost falls for it, and then he sees the crease in the corner of her mouth. He smiles and sips his coffee.

It takes a little over an hour to cross the island of Funen. The bridge to Jutland peeks over the horizon, a few kilometres before the Little Belt of water they must cross to the mainland. Emma pretends to hold her breath as they drive up and over the bridge, and then splutters with laughter as Jon does the same.

"Stop it," she says, and slaps his arm. "You're driving."

"But if we breathe in the Jutland air, we might be infected."

Emma rolls down her window, and takes a long, deep breath of hot air.

"You'd better do the same, dad, before they figure out we're from Copenhagen."

"You think?"

"I do," she says with a definitive nod.

Jon winds down his window, breathes in, and then increases speed as the road from the bridge opens into three lanes of motorway. He fiddles with the GPS, taps the part of the screen that indicates they have another two-and-a-half hours before they arrive at their destination. Emma lowers the back of her seat and slides into a sleeping position, bare feet on the dashboard, her knees tucked into the seat in such a way that always makes Jon envious. Being too big and broad to be a comfortable passenger, he settles on driving.

"I might have to stop for another coffee," he says.

"Hmm."

Jon can almost hear Emma's music. He turns on the radio, finds *Radio 24/7* and uses the next kilometre to guess the topic of debate. He turns up the volume at the mention of the word *wolf*.

"My son saw a wolf when he was walking to the bus stop," a man says. Jon pictures him as a middle-aged teacher, the kind that are informed but often swayed by popular opinion, passionately naïve when pushed.

"And what was his reaction?" the presenter asks.

"He was scared, of course he was. There's been a lot of talk in the news, and we – my wife and I – told

Johan that he shouldn't worry, that the wolf, if he ever met one, would be more scared than he was. It would probably run away. That's what the wildlife experts say. He would be lucky to see one, we said."

"And was he?"

"What?"

"Do you think Johan was lucky to see a wolf?"

Jon turned up the volume in the pause before the man answered.

"It's a wonderful animal," the man says, "but I think we're *lucky* that nothing happened."

Jon sank back into his seat.

"What do you mean?"

"Well, it's just not suited to Denmark, is it? The wolf I mean. It's too big. It's a predator. We have laws about dangerous dogs, the kind they used to use for fighting."

"Pit bulls?"

"Yes, that kind of thing. They must be muzzled, kept on a lead. But the wolf can just run free – no muzzle, no leash. You're not even allowed to shoot it if it attacks."

"Do you think we should shoot it?"

"Maybe."

"Suppose you were a hunter, and you had been with Johan that day and you had your gun with you. Would you have shot the wolf?"

"Shot it, or shot at it?"

The presenter says nothing, and Jon turns up the volume for a second time.

"I would have shot it," the man says.

"To scare it away?"

"No. I would have killed it."

Jon turns off the radio. He rests his elbow on the

door, cups his chin in his hand, stares straight ahead and lets the car select the appropriate distance between the vehicles in front. The computer slows the car and Jon is trapped behind a car towing a caravan. There's a sticker on the back, it's a moose. The caravan is German, but the moose sticker, Jon knows, comes from Sweden. *They have wolves in Sweden*, he thinks, *and a lot of land.* Jon isn't the first to imagine that the problem with wolves in Denmark is that the country is too small. And yet, there are swathes of open land between the cities, towns and villages.

Farmland.

And that's the problem, he thinks.

Denmark is an agricultural land. *Venstre*, the Prime Minister's party, has been the farmers' party, for many generations. Jon understands why he has been asked to investigate. Felix's party needs an answer that the farmers will accept, that the farming community can implement, something to appease and placate the tight-knit communities that are far from the arrogant and distanced Copenhageners.

Jon sees a sign for a service station and slows to leave the motorway. Emma snores lightly in the passenger seat, and Jon lets her sleep. He rolls down the window a little, and then locks the car, before walking into the restaurant building. He buys a coffee, finds a table, and scans the faces of families, truck drivers, tourists – foreign and domestic. Any one of them could be from Jutland. So could he.

He sips his coffee, thinking about his decision to accept the politician's request.

"I could be in Greenland," he whispers, his breath stirring the surface of the coffee as he holds the mug close to his lips. "But I chose Jutland."

Jon lets his thoughts brew as he sits at the table, the slow spin of the fans in the ceiling pushing hot air around the room, together with the truck drivers' sweat, the baby's nappy, the coffee, the hot dog water and a faint smell of diesel as the automatic doors shush open and closed.

He remembers the words of the man on the radio, quoting the wildlife experts. Like many others, the man is used to listening to oft repeated guidelines and advice about what to do when encountering wolves in nature, or in a farmer's field by a bus stop on their way to school. What would he say to that man? What advice would he have?

As he sips his coffee he thinks about the wolf and how little he knows about its behaviour. He knows what it does in the wild, how it hunts for food, how it communicates – or, at least, how he *thinks* it communicates, but the wolves he knows about are the Arctic wolves of Northeast Greenland. The Grey Wolf of Europe is different. Most of the studies he has read on the behaviour of the Grey Wolf have been written about observations of wolves in captivity. But maybe the common denominator – regardless of which breed of wolf – is people. The wolf problem is a *people problem*.

"I have to learn about people," Jon says, louder than he intended. He smiles at the family sitting at the table next to him. Jon takes out his wallet, pulls a business card from the sleeve, and reads the name on the card: David McGrath, Wildlife Biologist, University of Alaska, Fairbanks. *David knows about people* and *wolves*, he thinks, reflecting on the strange conversation he had with the biologist when they met.

He taps one side of the card on the table, finishes

his coffee, slipping the card into his wallet as he stands up. Jon buys a drink and a sandwich for Emma, carries them to the car, and stops to look at his daughter as she yawns and stretches in the passenger seat. She tugs the ear buds from her ears and smiles back at him.

"What?" she mouths, as he smiles.

Two Copenhageners in Jutland, he thinks, as he opens the car door. *Two sheep among the wolves.*

Chapter 7

Like the rest of the congregation, Bo Falk is hot. The sweat drips down the back of his neck, he feels it beading in his hair, collecting on his forehead. He would wipe it if it wasn't for the look Aage Dahl gives him from where he stands at the elevated pulpit. *It's not enough that the church sits on the highest point around Thyrup*, Bo thinks, *the shepherd must be higher than his flock, always.* Bo holds the priest's gaze, pushes his thoughts to one side, and listens.

"Werewolves are among us," Aage says and waits for a suitable response. Perhaps it is the heat, but there is barely a ripple of emotion in the pews. He continues. "That's what I might have said if I was a priest a few hundred years ago. You won't believe it, but in the dark ages, before we were enlightened, skin disease, disability, sickness, all these things could be attributed to werewolves. A child's broad forehead, small ears and wide mouth, for example, might have been the result of a disability, but in those days they were more likely to think it was due to the pairing of a woman and a werewolf. Who was to know any different? Who dared to argue, to offer an alternative explanation? No, better to let things take their course, better to burn the werewolf at the stake, or the woman, to prevent her being fooled once more. The wolf lived among us, then as now."

Aage takes a sip of water, turns the page of his sermon, and continues.

"Now, I see among us today those of you who suffer still, those who see the wolf as a predator, preying on the weak. If the drought was not enough, you wonder why God has sent the wolf. Why now, when you are on your knees, does he send the beast to make you grovel lower still?" Aage hides a smile behind another sip of water. He sees the reaction, the frowns, and the questioning glances his flock sends to one another. "Too much?" he asks. "Too dramatic?" He leans over the pulpit. "Not for the farmer sent begging to the bank to feed his family. Not to the family wondering if it is safe to let their children walk to school. Should they risk being late for work to drive their children past the bus stop, past the fields, right to the school gate. Perhaps they should walk with them all the way to the classroom?"

Aage nods as the organist gestures at the door. Once it is open, a warm breeze drifts through the church. It barely flutters the pages of Aage's sermon, but he pauses all the same, as the tiny lick of wind eases his congregation, lifting the corners of mouths, cooling brows, bringing hope.

"You're worried," he says. "And you have every right to worry, but you must not fear, for there is always hope, just as there was hope then, in the time of werewolves. No, Tommy," Aage says, as he catches the wide-eyes of a boy in the front row, "I am not going to burn anyone at the stake. Unless," he says, "you've been teasing your sister, again."

"I haven't," Tommy says, and the church is filled with soft laughter.

Aage lets them settle, takes another sip of water, followed by a dramatic gripping of the sides of the pulpit.

"It's true that our opinions are divided across our fair land. I do not share the opinions of my colleagues in Odense, Aarhus, and certainly not Copenhagen."

Another flutter of laughter.

"But we are all united in the idea of community. A community for all. Even here, today, I see Danes, I see our friends from Germany, I see Andreas Stenberg wondering when I will be finished so he can open the store and sell some ice-cream. Am I right, Andreas?"

"Yes," he says, and shrugs.

Aage laughs alongside his congregation, feels the lifting of spirits, knows this is where he wants and needs them to be, to bring the community together.

"Together we are strong. Together we are a community, and our doors are open to all who need our help, all who want our help, and even those who have neither needs nor wants. I am talking about the animals, the birds, the dwellers of the hedgerows, the fish in our sea, and the hedgehogs in our gardens. They are a part of our community. They have their own needs and wants and, where we can, we provide for them, and they, in their own way, give back what they can. The hedgehog brings a smile to an adult's face, sparks wonder in a child's eyes as it snuffles and rustles through the undergrowth. We see the deer that graze in the fields from our cars early in the morning, or at twilight. The deer are royalty and their gifts are majestic, for who among you has not enjoyed venison, new potatoes, and mother-in-law's brown sauce?" Aage pauses to smile and nod at the reciprocating nudges and nods in the pews below him. "But there is one animal that we take no pleasure from. We can't eat it – even if it was legal to shoot it. We can't fence it in, or out," he says and looks at Bo. "There is no pleasure to be gained in its lope across the fields – we know it is up to no good. Even its fur is cowardly, camouflaging its true intent, to take, to steal, to kill."

Bo looks down as Camilla takes his hand. He squeezes her fingers, just once, strokes her soft hand with the coarse skin of his thumb, and then Aage's words draw him back to the sermon.

"The wolf is among us. It is not God's creation; it is the work of the Devil, a beast on our lands. The wolf is among us, and yet, it does not belong, it never has. But now it is up to you. It's your turn to act. Come to the meeting on Wednesday. Sign the petition. It is time to uncloak the wolf. Lead bullets are against the law, but lead," he says, and lifts a pencil from the pulpit, "will save our community. Sign the petition. Protect your community. And now," he says, sinking his shoulders, lowering his hands, "turn to page two-hundred-and-ninety-three in your hymn books: *A shepherd never forgets his sheep*."

Bo mouths the words that his wife sings so clearly. He leans forwards, catches Jacob's eye, and returns his son's grin. Aage had promised werewolves, and he delivered, filling the minds of his flock with demonic images of the wolf, although, if he is honest, Bo is more afraid of the German Shepherd dog who is now in the barn at the Falk family farm.

He turns the page, finds his place, and sings a little louder, and the growling of the dog at the end of its long, rusted chain recedes, just a little.

The breeze filtering into the church is stronger outside. The Danish flag is bright red, crossed with white against a beryl blue sky.

After the service, Bo finds Viktoria arranging cornflowers beside her father's gravestone. He waits as she pushes the last long stem into a thin robust vase.

"They were his favourite," she says, as she stands.

"They are a weed."

"A pretty weed. He would stop harvesting if he found a patch of them."

"I know," Bo says. "I saw him do it more than once. It made no sense to me."

"Not everything does."

Viktoria looks around Bo's shoulder. Aage stands at the entrance to the church, and she forces a smile when he catches her eye.

"Thank you," Bo says, "for what you said to Tilde. It means a lot."

"Does it?" Viktoria scuffs the gravel on her father's grave with the tips of her shoes. "I did it for my father, not for you. But I don't know what he would have wanted. I don't know what I want."

"He would have done the same. He had sheep too."

"But he loved nature," she says, and gestures at the cornflowers.

"You're saying I don't?"

"I'm saying the wolf is a part of nature. Not the demon that Aage makes him out to be."

"It *was* a bit dramatic."

"Straight out of the 1700s. I don't know what he was thinking," she says. "Noah almost came to church today. I'm glad he didn't."

"But he'll be at the meeting on Wednesday?"

"Maybe. Anton's combine has broken down again. Noah's waiting for parts. If they arrive on Wednesday, he won't come. He'll be busy."

"Anton never mentioned it."

"That's a surprise."

"What does that mean?"

Viktoria waits for a German family to pass; mother and father and young son. The boy is giddy about werewolves, while the mother sends furrowed looks towards the church.

"There's a reason Anton wasn't at church today. He's not like you. He's definitely not like his father," she says, and glances at Aage. "You've never wondered why he chose to take his mother's maiden name?"

"I heard rumours. Aage doesn't talk about it."

"But Anton knows when Aage has been to the see the Falks, stirring up trouble."

"Is that what he thinks?"

Viktoria shrugs.

Bo remembers when one of Anton's bullocks was attacked a few years ago. The papers said it was a dog and Anton said so too. Bo struggles to remember exactly when it was, and he doesn't remember when he last had a long talk with Anton. The drought has kept them busy. They barely have time for a few words when they pass in the store. *He should have told me about the combine*, he thinks.

"It's the wolf," Viktoria says. "It's dividing the community. And that sermon didn't help." She nods at the church. A second later, she drifts away from Bo.

The breeze is stronger now, blowing from the sea, lifting the salt tang from the waves and brushing the roofs and windows with fine crystals. Denmark is suffering. Inland farms are drying out faster than those along the coast. *Thyrup has some luck*, Bo thinks. But Thyrup has the wolf, and the environmentalists, the academics, and the so-called elite, sitting high on their morals, looking down, look from afar, from

Copenhagen. Christiansborg is a long way from Thyrup. They are at opposite ends of the country, almost parallel, on a direct line, but poles apart. They might as well be north and south.

Bo thinks of Belgium, and the headquarters of the European Union. He wonders how decisions that affect his fate in the jaws of the wolf can be made by the people who are so remote from his life, his country.

"Experts," Aage says, as he joins Bo beside the grave of Viktoria's father.

"What?"

"They are sending experts from Christiansborg. One, at least. A man and his daughter. They will be staying at the nature commission house, the one down by the beach."

"How do you know?"

"Tilde Sørensen," Aage says, and smiles. "She called the ministry for a comment, and the minister, Felix Poulsen, said he was sending a wolf expert to Thyrup. Can you believe it?"

"What will he do?"

"Investigate, I suppose." Aage gestures at the gate. "I need a smoke. Walk with me."

Bo sees Camilla and Jacob talking with Anton and his wife, Maja. He doesn't remember seeing them in church. They must have arrived after the sermon. He wants to talk to his neighbour, but feels compelled to linger and to share a cigarette with the priest, to listen to what the old man has to say.

Old, he thinks, but wise in Thyrup ways.

"I'm very fond of you, Bo. You and your family," Aage says. "It's not just Camilla's buttermilk."

"No?" Bo forces a laugh, but his eyes are on

Anton.

"Did you pick up the dog?"

"Yes," Bo says.

"And?"

"It's wild. I'm not a dog person."

"You don't have to be. It just has to do its job."

"Protecting the sheep."

"Protecting the community, Bo. This is bigger than the Falk farm. You know that."

"Do you want me to loan out the dog? Is that it? I'm worried enough about having it on my own land."

"The dog will be fine," Aage says. "Besides, you need it to be wild. It needs to scare away the wolves."

Bo watches the priest, as Aage finishes his cigarette.

"Was that a riddle?" he asks. "Because the way you said *wolves* made me think you meant something else."

"You worry too much, Bo. It's wearing you down. Let me take some of that worry. It is the shepherd's burden, after all."

Chapter 8

Jon wakes early on Monday morning, Emma is still sleeping. The *little house by the sea*, as Emma calls it, is a dune's width from the beach. The lapping of the waves, the shush of wind, and the sand drifting across the beach, reminds Jon of Greenland. The Thyrup beach is broad, pitted with historical bunkers, a reminder of the German occupation, now decorated with Jutland's answer to street art – a graffiti whale here, a troll there, a wolf's paw.

Jon stares at the paw. He should be buying breakfast; the kitchen is bare. But the paw and the words arcing around it consume him. *Wild* and *free* the words say, the paint tacky – either fresh or blistered by the sun. Someone, perhaps a visitor, drifting through, has captured the Thyrup mood. *Someone* speaks for the wolf, but the wolf is silent.

The path from the beach house is narrow. Jon passes his car, continues to the road, and sees the sign hanging above the entrance of the local store, *Thyrup Dagli'Brugs*. It is cooler inside, and there is a small bustle around the bakery counter where breakfast rolls are buttered and bagged for tourists. The locals visit the bakery on Sundays, but the store is busy, and will be until sometime in October, when the German cars are outnumbered by the Danes as they enjoy the autumn half-term.

Jon won't be here in October. He is as much a tourist as the Germans waiting for breakfast rolls. He joins the queue, waits for his rolls, and places them in the basket, carrying them around the store as he finds what they need for breakfast. He yawns, struggling still with the jetlag from Alaska, and the drive from

Copenhagen.

"Jon Østergård?" a man says, offering a gnarled hand in greeting.

"Yes."

"My name is Aage Dahl, the local priest. Welcome to Thyrup."

"You know my name," Jon says.

"Of course," Aage says, and points a nicotine finger at the ceiling. He winks as Jon's frown creases his brow. "I'm kidding. Tilde Sørensen told me your name, but you won't know her either."

"No."

"She's the local journalist. About to hit the big time too," Aage says, as he steers Jon towards the refrigerators at the back of the store. "You'll need milk and cheese to go with those rolls."

"Thanks," Jon says.

"Of course, rumour has it you are not the only newcomer arriving in Thyrup today. DR is sending a TV crew, and the local station too." Aage leans closer to whisper, "They are staying for a few days at least. It looks like they are going on a safari." He winks. "Looking for wolves."

"That's why I'm here. But you know that."

"I do. And I want to invite you to a meeting on Wednesday. It will be a good time for you to get to know the Thyrup community. I'm quite sure everyone will be there, as *everyone* has an interest in the wolf, not just the journalists."

"Perhaps you can tell me who to talk to, before the meeting?"

"Bo Falk comes to mind," Aage says.

"He's the farmer in the article?"

"That's right. Although, he's busy right now.

They all are. It's the drought. There's a fire risk, you see. A single spark from a combine harvester, when the blades hit a rock, can set a whole field ablaze. We only have a voluntary fire brigade, you understand. Some of the farmers have converted tractors – the ones they use to spray crops – they have turned them into fire engines. It's that dry."

The view from the airplane over Zealand revealed a dry, yellow land. Jon wonders what he would have seen if he had flown to Jutland. The word *tinderbox* springs to his mind, and he thinks about the priest's words as he chooses a carton of milk from the fridge.

"Of course," Aage says, "the sea isn't faring much better."

"The sea?"

"Algae," he says. "It's blooming. They say you shouldn't swim. So now we have fields where nothing grows, and what does grow can burst into flame. We have tourists on the beach looking for shade, looking to cool down, but they can't swim, can't even paddle. They are moving on, to campsites further and further up the coast, just a kilometre or so ahead of the algae." Aage pauses to shrug. "On top of all that, we have the wolf."

"You paint quite a picture," Jon says.

"If I was wont to use an idiom – and we Danes do like our idioms – well, I might say it was time to paint the devil on the wall. Ironic, I know," Aage says, with a grin. "I'm a priest."

Jon lowers the basket to the floor. He was tired before, but the priest's account of the Thyrup situation drains him.

"Are you alright, Jon?"

"I'm sorry," he says. "I didn't think it was that

bad."

"Thyrup is a small farming community. People are either farming or support the farming industry, such as tractor mechanics like Noah, the vet's husband. Others are in the tourist trade. Lots of farms have a bed and breakfast; some of them even have a small campsite. Thyrup depends on the land and sea. The algae will disappear again, but the wolf is here to stay. You didn't ask for my opinion, but you need to know, our visitors are not wolf-watchers. They have come here for the nature, and if they don't feel safe walking in the woods, they will go somewhere else, and Thyrup will dwindle and die."

It's no coincidence that the priest was waiting for Jon to come to the store. It is an ambush, a first strike, and it works. Jon thinks about the priest's words all the way back to the beach house. He is quiet as he lays the small folding table for breakfast, feels the sand grating the soles of his feet as he pads barefoot up the wooden stairs to knock on his daughter's bedroom door. She murmurs something that suggests she might get up soon, and Jon is left with his thoughts as the sun beats down on the thatch roof. He wonders how much of a spark it would take to ignite the thatch and is thankful neither he nor his daughter smokes.

Despite Aage's suggestion that Jon speak to the farmer, it is the veterinarian he wants to visit first. He leaves a note for Emma, as well as some money on top of the list of things she should buy, when or *if* she surfaces for breakfast. He pulls the Tilde Sørensen article from the folder Felix gave him before they left Christiansborg and makes a note of the name of the veterinarian. He could have asked Aage. He looks her up on the Internet, then pockets his smartphone and grabs the keys to his car.

The tractors, long trailers, and giant wheels of the combine harvesters encourage Jon to drive as close to the verge as possible. But the roads in Jutland are perilous, the verges disappear into deep troughs designed to catch the run-off from the fields and the roads. Jon almost smiles at the thought. But the lack of rain is just as threatening as the idea of flooding or the cloudbursts that are common in spring.

As he drives towards the vet's house he spots smoke on the horizon. He slows as he passes a field with a single fire engine and a bustle of farmers, farm hands, men and women, beating at the flames with the broad rubber fans of fire beaters. He pulls up on the side of the road, parking as close to the drainage ditch as possible and jogs across the tinder field. Once there, he grabs a beater from the bed of a pickup truck and joins the line of soot-smeared Thyrup folk, beating back the flames as the volunteers of the local fire brigade douse a blazing combine harvester with water.

The flames lick at the field. Sometimes, when the oxygen is beaten away by a farm hand, the flames disappear underground, smouldering in the stem of dry grass, licking at the roots, emerging again when the beater moves on, feeding off the air seeping into the porous earth. Jon tires quickly, his brow black, smoke in his lungs. The firemen turn their hoses from the black combine. The metal ticks in the heat as they douse the field with the last litres of water from the tank. The hose sputters and the water is gone. The firemen beat from the other side of the farmers, working towards them, as they pinch the flames between them. A single flame crackles behind Jon, and he turns to beat it out and finally the fire is extinguished. The firemen toss bottles of water to the beaters from the cab of the fire engine, and they drink, their mouths and chins washed pink and white in dribbles of water streaking black faces.

"Thank you," a man says, and slaps Jon's shoulder.

"You're welcome."

"You're not from around here."

"You can tell?"

The man laughs. "My name is Anton Bjerg. This is my field. The combine belongs to a friend. At least it did."

"Østergård," Jon says, and takes another slug of water.

"The wolf guy?"

"I suppose so."

Anton wipes his mouth with the back of his hand, nods at the pickup. Jon walks beside him as the beaters inspect the burned soles of their shoes, drink more water, and sweat in the heat.

"There's rumour of a den," Anton says. "No-one knows where, or if they do, they're not saying."

"Do you have an idea?"

"An *idea*, yes, but not an exact location. We're trying to clear the fields," he says, and waves his hand at the black stumps of wizened wheat. "I've been a little busy. Everyone has. Do you have a piece of paper?"

"Yes," Jon says, as Anton takes a pen from the dashboard of the pickup.

"We're here," he says, and draws a square field on the paper. He draws the road, more fields, another road, and a circle with a cross in it. "The church."

"Right."

"This is my land." Anton draws diagonal lines across his fields. "This is my neighbour, Bo Falk. Somewhere between these fields is the den," he says, and draws an oval covering one of his fields and two of Bo's. "This is a wooded area. It's perfect for a den, with old beech trees and soil banks sloping between thick roots."

"Other people must know about the wood."

"They do. Lots of people have looked, and I think that's why we haven't seen anything. There's just too much activity. Now, we've had some fires, the tourist season has entered the busy period, people have other things to do. If it wasn't for Bo's sheep, and my dad's sermon, the wolf might have been forgotten, at least until the end of the summer."

"Your dad is Aage Dahl?"

"You've met him?"

"He found me at the store this morning."

Anton laughs. "Of course. He knew you were coming."

"So, you think I should look in the wood?"

"You're the expert."

"In Greenland maybe," Jon says, and smiles. "I know about the Arctic wolf, the white ones. There are no trees in Northeast Greenland. The dens I found were beneath rocks."

Anton shrugs. "Well, I don't know about that, but that's my best bet."

"I'm curious. Why are you telling me? I mean, you're a…"

"Farmer? I am. I keep a few head of dairy cattle. Nothing much. Crops are my main investment."

Anton pauses to look at his field. "It was my main investment. But, maybe I'm naïve or perhaps I just have a bad sense for figures, but I think that a bullock here and there is just the natural cost of doing business."

"A bullock?"

"Yeah, one of my bullocks was attacked a few years ago. I told the papers it was a dog. It could have been, but I'm pretty sure it was a wolf." Anton folds the paper with the roughly drawn map and hands it to Jon. "Don't tell anyone about the den. Nothing good will come of it. Not in Thyrup."

Chapter 9

Tuesday is Emma's day. It was a condition Jon had to agree to on the first night in the beach house, before she crashed in her bed. Tuesday – her non-vegetarian day – starts with Emma's favourite breakfast bacon, thick, English style. They run an hour later along the beach, with Jon doing his best to keep up. Finally, the heat beats them off the beach and into a café for ice-cream.

"I haven't changed my mind," Emma says, as she twists a chunk of mint chocolate from the scoop of ice-cream melting at the top of the cone. "The shops still sell crappy things at shitty prices."

Jon reminds her of this when she buys a pair of sunglasses and a new cover for her iPhone.

"I can't help it if they hide good stuff in-between."

"No," Jon says. "Of course not."

He picks out a pair of sunglasses for himself, the mirrored kind, wondering if he wore them backwards he could erase the image of his daughter in her cropped denims, short enough to start more fires, and her bikini top. Emma's long dark hair was tousled in a bun, with wayward strands blowing in the slight onshore breeze. If nothing else, the glasses might scare off any young men foolish enough to approach Emma on the beach, Emma on the streets of Thyrup, Emma *anywhere*.

"You didn't tell me about the fire," she says, as they walk into the centre of Thyrup.

"I was tired."

"And sooty. There's a handprint on the bathroom door."

"I'll clean it off later."

"Sure," Emma says. She slows outside another art studio, the coastline is peppered with them. But she is not interested in art. It was the glimpse she caught of the boy with surfer hair across the street that made her think that Thyrup isn't quite as dead as she first thought. "I'll see you back at the house, dad."

"Where are you going?"

"Investigating," she says, and pulls her glasses down to give her father a conspiratorial wink. "Do you trust me?"

"I suppose I have to."

"It *is* my day," she says. She waggles the phone in her hand. "You can always call me."

Emma leaves her dad outside the art studio, jogs across the narrow street and enters the store. She tugs off her glasses and hangs them from the centre clasp of her bikini. The aisles are tightly spaced, filled by shop assistants stocking the shelves in the brief lull between lunch and late afternoon. Emma sees the boy, about her age, squinting at a list in his hand. He's standing by the refrigerators. She can feel the cool air pressing against her skin as she stands next to him.

"Hello," she says, flashing one of her *Instagram* smiles. Her predator smile, tested under fire, on more than one occasion – she knows it is a killer. The boy falters, his jaw drops just a little, and Emma feels the corners of her eyes crease. She focuses on his pupils, sees them widen, and allows herself to blush. *I overdid it*, she thinks, as the boy fumbles to close the refrigerator.

"Jacob," he says, after a long pause.

"Emma."

"You're a tourist?"

"Kind of," she says.

"Not from round here."

"Copenhagen."

"Right."

Jacob drops his list as he picks up the basket. A strand of Emma's hair brushes his cheek as she bends down to pick up the list. She turns it one way and then the other, squinting until it makes sense.

"You need bread," she says.

"Yes."

"That's…"

"This way," he says, and nods towards the entrance. "At the bakery."

Emma sees her dad across the street as she waits beside Jacob in the line at the bakery. She shoos Jon away with a flick of her hand, relishing for a second the fact that this is her father's worst nightmare – Emma meeting a strange young man in wildest Jutland. But she's pretty certain that Jacob is a lamb compared to the boys in Copenhagen, who knows what her father would think he if ever saw the photos on her phone, or even talked to one of her friends. The initiation ceremonies and the Gymnasium parties were always wild, usefully, they always seemed to coincide with field trips to Greenland.

"Imagine that," she whispers.

"What?"

"Nothing." Emma gives Jacob the list. "It just says rye bread."

"It's for my dad. He doesn't like the stuff mum makes – too many seeds. Every time I buy him another loaf of bread, he owes me, see?"

"You're blackmailing your father?"

Jacob shrugs.

"Genius," she says, and gives Jacob another point for initiative, as she steps back to covertly check out his body.

Emma's friends always laugh when she attempts this. It's as if she has never really grasped the meaning of the word covert, she always seems to forget the C. But Emma knows it's all part of the game. *Besides*, she always says, *why should men get away with looking. If I'm checking someone out, they need to* know *I'm checking them out.* Jacob knows, she's sure of it. The only question is what will he do next?

Emma realises she's not going to find out, because the next moment her dad walks into the store. She glares at him for a second, catches the look on his face, and then nods as he beckons for her to follow him outside.

"It was nice meeting you, Jacob," Emma says. She has just enough composure to blast him with another indecipherable smile, and then she is out on the street, and her father thrusts his phone into her hand.

"Your mum," he says, and starts walking towards the beach house.

"Hi," Emma says, pulling a face as she follows her father. "Yes," she says, "this is my day."

Emma had always understood what her parents had in common, but she struggled for a long time to understand what pushed them apart. In her darkest moments she thought it might be her, that she had done something. Other times she thought it might be about wolves. They had always fought over theories, like typical academics, backs to the wall, flinging theories at each other, flourishing field notes, running fingers across scrawled observations in tattered and mildewed diaries. Emma read some of the notes once, when the books were abandoned, and her parents had called a truce and disappeared for an hour to a nearby restaurant with peace and harmony on the menu. In the notes Emma read about alpha males and alpha females. She dug into books like Barry Lopez' *Of Wolves and Men* or L. David Mech's *The Wolf*, reading highlighted sections on behaviour, collated observations from experts in the field, paragraphs detailing the female role in hunting and leading the pack. That was when she knew her parents were both Alphas. That was when she stopped reading about wolves. The more she read, the more she understood. Jon and Elin were wolves, and they needed to lead.

It just didn't make any sense. If the wolves could find a balance, a means of understanding each other's role, why couldn't her parents? Clearly, it was a human problem. It had nothing to do with wolves. That was when Emma stopped reading.

These thoughts help Emma coast through the conversation with her mother. They had an agreement that Elin called when she could, and Emma made the time to talk, as long as she wasn't in class. There were times, such as right now, when Emma regretted the agreement and wondered if there was a way around it.

"When you've graduated," Jon says, as Emma hands him the phone. "If you're lucky."

"It's like it's a control thing. I have to drop what I'm doing and answer her call."

"She's busy, Emma. That's all."

"What if I'm busy? What then? And who are they?"

She points at a couple tucked into the shade

beneath a corner of thatch on the beach house. The man looks like a hippy, and the woman, older than him, could be his older lover. She gives them names as they walk the last hundred metres to the house and is disappointed when they introduce themselves with far more ordinary names than she imagined.

"Sebastian Ibsen," the man says, holding out his hand towards Jon.

"Olivia Johansen," the woman says. "You're the wolf man."

Emma sniggers. Part of her hopes the woman is joking, but the glint in her eyes suggests something more sinister. Emma unlocks the door and Jon invites them inside.

"What can I do for you?" he asks, gesturing for them to sit down.

Emma places a bottle of cold water on the table, finds four glasses in the cupboard and then curls her legs beneath her bottom on the sofa. She brushes sand from her feet and studies the woman as the woman studies her dad. Sebastian is the first to speak.

"We think you need our help," he says. "The people in Thyrup are…"

"You're not from Thyrup?"

"No," Olivia says.

"But we've been here a few months now. We have a good grasp of the situation, and we're ready to act."

"Seb," Olivia says.

"It's alright," he says. "Jon is one of us, he's on our side."

"Everybody seems to know my name," Jon says. He catches Emma's eye and she raises her eyebrows.

I'll just sit here and keep quiet, she thinks. *Let dad do his thing.*

"We heard you were coming," Olivia says. "But we've also read your thesis."

"Arctic Wolves and the Art of Denning in Greenland," Sebastian says. "You called denning an *art.*"

"Thanks," Jon says, "but what did you mean about sides?"

"The side of the wolf. That's why you're here, isn't it?" Sebastian looks at Olivia. "To protect the wolf."

Emma studies Olivia's face and recognises the look of the alpha, but a different kind to her mother. Despite all their arguments, her parents always made up, until the day they didn't, when they realised that neither of them would ever *win*. But from the look in Olivia's eye, Emma guesses she isn't the type to give in, ever. Sebastian knows it too.

"Look," Jon says, "let's start again." He pours water into the glasses. "I'm here to assess the situation, to get a feeling for what's going on, and to make recommendations based on my observations. I don't get to decide the fate of the wolf. I'm not here to protect it, but I'm not here to kill it either."

"But you will make recommendations?"

"Based on my observations, yes." Jon stands up and gives Emma a glass of water. "It's hot," he says. "Three litres a day."

Emma sips her water, knowing that she doesn't have space in her body for three litres of water a day. *He's been reading the news again*, she thinks, and shifts her position. The sand from her toes is now beneath her thighs. She brushes it away as Sebastian starts to speak.

"The government will listen to you. If we can prove that the wolf is innocent…"

"Innocent?" Jon wishes David McGrath was sitting beside him at the table. "There is no *innocent* in the world of wolves. They don't have laws, they just do what they have to do, what they have always done. You can't use human concepts like *innocent* or *guilty*. It just doesn't work that way."

"But those are the concepts that people use," Olivia says. "If you don't prove the wolf is innocent, they will find it guilty."

"They already have," Sebastian says. Emma sees the look Olivia gives him, and is not surprised when he lowers his eyes, and turns his head.

"Are you going to the meeting tomorrow?" Olivia asks.

"I've been invited," Jon says. "I think it is appropriate to go."

"Then you'll see for yourself," she says.

Emma stays seated as the woman stands up and tells Sebastian that they are leaving. She waits until they are gone, the door is shut, and her father joins her on the sofa.

"What do you think?" he says.

"Definitely an alpha."

"Yep, she's trouble."

"Dad," Emma says, "show me someone in Thyrup who *isn't* trouble."

"I will, when I meet them."

Chapter 10

Thyrup shares a mini sports hall with the neighbouring villages of Althum and Vedeså, and residents from all three communities pack the hall, sitting in rows in front of folding tables, and a hastily-erected screen. Jon shushes Emma before she comments on the third technical hitch in a row, as he waits for his turn to speak. There is an agenda, and, in the time it takes to connect the computer to the projector, Jon asks Aage why his name is not on the list of speakers.

"I have my own meetings," he says, "every Sunday at nine o'clock. You and your daughter are most welcome."

"Of course."

"And," Aage says, just as the screen flickers into life, "don't think I didn't hear about the fire in the field. People are talking about what you did. My son, is very grateful."

Jon nods as the chairman of the meeting expresses his delight at the turn-out, runs through the agenda and appeals for a positive tone throughout the meeting.

"You've probably seen the comments on Facebook, and I think you'll agree that everybody is entitled to an opinion, even if your neighbour doesn't agree with it. Although," he says, as looks around the hall, "unless you have fake profiles, I think most of the comments are from people outside of Thyrup. It seems the country is divided, and the line has been drawn here, right through our community."

Jon looks around the hall, sees the people leaning against the walls, standing by the door, and even spilling out of the entrance. All the doors are open, hands are waved in front of faces, agendas folded and flapped. There is sweat on his daughter's brow, and, when he leans forwards, his shirt clings to the back of the seat. Perhaps the only saving grace of the drought is the lack of mosquitoes.

The first speaker introduces the purpose of the Society for a Wolf-Free Denmark, and Jon listens. He squints at the screen and chooses to scroll through the list of points on the society's website on his phone instead. He ignores the links but lingers over the concerns raised about Denmark being too small a country to accommodate the wolf. According to the society, wolves will regularly be within a few hundred metres of houses, farms, towns. If they are not allowed to protect their land, livestock, pets and their children, then the wolves will be too close. The speaker raises the same points and around Jon and Emma heads bob in agreement, together with muffled murmurs of approval.

Emma pokes her father's leg and points discreetly towards the far wall. He sees Olivia and Sebastian glowering at the speaker. *They must be in the minority*, he thinks, and takes a quick look at the exits, gauges the distance, and leans back in his seat.

"What are you doing?" Emma whispers.

"Looking for a way out."

"It's a bit late for that," Aage says, as he leans over. "It's your turn to speak."

Jon looks up, as the chair for the meeting beckons to him. Low voices ripple like a wave across the seats as Jon squeezes his way to the front of the hall. He takes heart when he hears comments about his actions in the burning field, only to sink again at the venom wrapped around the title *government man*. He doesn't turn to see who said it.

The lights are brighter at the front of the hall, the microphone sweaty in his hand. He faces the crowd, smiles when he sees Emma, and begins.

"My name is Jon Østergård. I am a wildlife biologist. I study wolves."

For just a second, he imagines the crowd might say *"Hi, Jon"*, but it's not that kind of meeting, and Jon realises his jokes and casual approach won't work here. Nor will he draw attention to his daughter. He wishes he had never brought her here. He wishes they were back in Copenhagen, or Alaska, anywhere but Thyrup. In this crowd, the hatred is barely contained beneath a thin layer of skin – he's never experienced anything like it. Emma can feel it too, he can see that. He wants to tell her to leave, he wishes there was some signal he could send, and then he looks at Aage, nods at him, and takes a breath as the priest raises his hands, ever so slightly. If Aage is here, if he sits by Emma, she is safe. Jon coughs to clear his throat and starts again.

"You're wondering why I'm here?"

"Are you here to kill those bloody wolfs?" a woman shouts.

"Astrid?" the chairman says, as he takes the microphone from Jon. "Please."

"Well," says a portly man in the second row. "Are you?"

"Let him speak, Levi," the chairman says.

"It's okay," Jon says. He takes the microphone from the chairman's hand. "I'm not here to kill the wolves."

"Then why are you here?" Levi says.

"I've come to assess the situation."

"You don't need to assess anything. we can tell you how it is," says a grey-haired woman towards the back. She stands up. "We've got wolves, and we want rid of them."

"I understand, but it's just not that simple."

"It's simple enough to shoot the bastard wolf," Levi says. "All you need is a gun."

Jon looks at Emma as both of them sense the emotional charge among the people in all the rows, rippling around the walls. Comments are hurled, incidents stated, and… Jon freezes as he sees the empty chair beside Emma. The priest is gone. She is alone, among the wolves. And then Aage is there again, one hand around Jon's shoulder, and another plucking the microphone from his hand.

"Please," he says. "Quiet now."

Jon's throat is dry. He wonders how he can speak as the people settle, brows are mopped, shirts are plucked from breasts and chests. Emma has curled her knees to her body, perched her heels on the edge of her seat. She's not nineteen anymore. There's a wild sheen to her eyes, and Jon looks at her as he grasps the microphone. He thinks he's whispering, but the words boom through the speakers as the crowd hushes.

"Are you okay?"

She nods.

"Okay," he says.

Aage steps to one side. The man is a ward against evil, and Jon resists the urge to shuffle closer to him.

"The Minister for Environment and Food asked me to come to Thyrup to find out about the wolves. He wants to know…" Jon pauses as a camera crew bumps their equipment through the crowd at the door. He recognises the woman, Lærke Wang, from *Danmarks Radio*. They start filming as Jon speaks. "I'm to gather information and write a report. I am going to make recommendations…"

"We don't need recommendations," Astrid says. "Just give us the means to protect ourselves."

"Kill the wolf," Levi shouts. "Kill them all."

"They don't belong here," another shouts.

"Denmark's too small," someone at the back of the hall calls out.

Aage lifts his hand to calm his flock, but his authority melts in the heat. Jon sees a young man push past rows of knees towards Emma, and he takes a step forwards, stopping when he recognises the boy from the store. The wild look in Emma's eyes softens as the boy asks if he can sit next to her, and then the people settle once more, and a hush descends on the hall. Jon turns to see who it is that has calmed the crowd – who is more powerful than the priest.

"Bo Falk," the man says, and shakes Jon's hand. "Can I?" He nods at the microphone.

"Yes," Jon says.

Bo settles the crowd with one deep breath. Sweat stains his shirt collar black as he draws the thick, hot air of the hall into his lungs. Like an exorcist he draws anger from the crowd and absorbs it. If the priest rules from a hilltop, Bo Falk leads in the trenches. The priest might be the shepherd of his flock, but Bo is the haggard sheep dog, with deep scars that speak louder than words.

And now they listen.

"Anton's field burned on Monday. You remember," he says. "Levi, you would have seen the smoke. Did you come?" Bo stares at Levi, lifts his eyes and finds Astrid at the back of the hall. "You live so close, Astrid, you would have smelled the smoke. Did you come? Did you beat back the flames? This man did. A stranger. He stopped on the road. Ran across the fields, grabbed a beater… He fought the flames, side by side with Anton, side by side with Thyrup folk." Bo lowers the microphone, looks around the room. "Let him speak," he says, and presses the microphone into Jon's hand.

Jon waits for Bo to sit down. Aage retreats to a seat beside the chairman, and then Jon is alone. He feels safer, if only for a moment. He tries a new tack.

"I know wolves," he says, "but I don't know people. I don't think I can make any recommendations before I get to know you. That's why I'm here." He pauses and wipes his brow. "But, if you don't mind, if you'll give me just a few minutes, let me tell you about the wolf, the one I know."

They listen for more than a few minutes, as Jon introduces them to the wolf. The wolf as father, the wolf as mother, hunter, babysitter, teacher, gatherer, fool and wise man, opportunist, glutton and survivor.

"A man once told me not to look where the wolf has been, but where he is going," he says. "If you'll show me where the wolf has been, if you'll let me into your homes, let me walk on your fields, maybe I can see where it is going." Jon lifts his hand as a man raises his. "Please, just a minute more. I don't mean where it is going to be tomorrow, or three weeks from now. I'm looking for patterns of anticipation." Jon thinks of a metaphor, something from the farming world. "It's like the buzzards that gather when you cut the corn," he says. "They start circling when the corn is already being cut. The wolf is different. He's smarter than your dog or cat. The wolf is one of the cleverer animals, as clever as a raven. I think the wolf would follow the combine harvester from the farm to the field. It might even know which field to go to as soon as it hears the combines."

There is a hush, even a nod or two between the older farmers, and their sons.

"You might be tempted to think that the wolf will return again and again to the same spot – like a field of sheep. Easy pickings. The shelf is always stocked. But they don't do that. They have a territory, one that expands, flexing with the flow of life, available food, weather conditions, rules, wolf law between packs, within its own pack. Their territory is huge. I'm sorry but fences will never work."

"What will?"

Jon looks for the speaker, finds the man with the raised hand, and shrugs.

"That's why I'm here. That's what I need to find out. Give me that chance, and I will take my recommendations to Christiansborg, directly to the minister. I can be your voice, if you let me, but," he raises his hand, "I am also the voice of the wolf. I wanted them to send a psychologist, but they sent me. I'm all you've got, so please, let me in."

Jon takes a business card from his wallet, hands it to the chairman.

"I'm staying at the beach house. The chairman has my number."

Jon hands the microphone to the chairman, nods at the priest, and looks around the room for the farmer. He walks towards the closest exist, slows as Emma works her way between the seats to join her father, tugging the young man by the hand behind her.

"Dad," she says, as they walk out of the hall and into the late light of the Danish summer evening, "I'd like you to meet Jacob."

"I'm Bo's son," he says, as he shakes Jon's hand. "Dad says you should come to supper."

Chapter 11

The lower boughs of the oak tree in the centre of the Falk family farm are bare of leaves. The first leaves to fall have blown away, leaving only prints in the dust on the cobblestones, temporary fossils like the tattoos pressed onto children's arms at the fair. Jon walks with Bo around the farm in the late evening light and Emma waves at him through the window of the farmhouse as she helps Jacob set the table for a late supper. The men come in shortly after and Bo shows Jon the aerial photograph of the farm mounted on the wall. It is faded, yellowed like the leaves, but the buildings are clear to see, and the tractor shines from the days when it was in its prime.

"It's almost as old as the farm," Bo says, with a thin smile.

"And the farm has been in your family…"

"Oh, I don't know, perhaps as far back as the late 1700s? There was a fire."

"Two fires," Camilla says.

"The farmhouse was rebuilt in 1926. Renovated later, just before we were married. But the Falks have farmed this area for a long time." Bo gestures at the table. "Let's eat."

The soup is thin and oily, meatballs and flour dumplings shaped like small fat thumbs bob on the surface. Camilla takes fresh bread rolls from the oven; the bread is warm, the butter thick, and Emma frowns after the first spoonful of soup.

"Is it alright?" Camilla asks.

She nods, swallows, and smiles.

"We usually have the frozen kind," she says. "Dad warms it up in the microwave."

"We have that too," Jacob whispers. "Mum's just showing off."

"Thank you, Jacob," Camilla says. "You're on dishes."

"I can help," Emma says.

Jacob leans closer to her, his surfer hair brushing the top of her arm. "The dishwasher is broken."

"Oh."

Camilla shares the last of the soup between Jacob and Emma, shooing them from the table with the dishes once they are finished. She makes fresh coffee, wipes the table, and watches the two men, as Bo opens an old photo album, the pages thick, burned at the edges, rescued from the second fire.

"This photo shows the field between the Bjerg farm and ours," Bo says, tapping a grainy image. He leans closer to read the pencil inscription beneath the photo. "It's from 1913. That's one hundred years after the last wolf was shot in Denmark, near Skive. But my father told stories about wolves around the Falk farm in the winter night, back in the days of my grandfather's grandfathers. Jacob used to sit on his knee and listen to stories about Falks and Bjergs with pitchforks and spears, a musket..." Bo smiles as he traces a blackened nail across the photo. "They fought the wolf here, apparently. On the Falk farm."

Jon smiles as Camilla places a mug of steaming coffee on the table. There is milk, cream and sugar, and a plate of biscuits that she quietly slides on to the table. She presses a finger to her lips and nods towards her son.

"Take one now," she whispers, "before he sees them."

The biscuit is thick, and it crumbles between

Jon's fingers as he bites into it and as Bo turns the page to another grainy image of the old Falk farm. Both men pause at a low bestial whine that presses against the windows at the back of the farmhouse, and for a moment the sound of the crickets is lost, and the darkness of an older time fires the imagination. Jon tilts his head to one side, waits for another whine, but it's lost, carried away by a sudden sea breeze, salty and sharp, stirring the heat.

Jon turns his head at a crash of plates by the sink and sees Emma, sweat on her brow, hair plastered to her cheeks, as she wipes hot plates with a damp teacloth. He doesn't think he has ever seen such a sight, and he smiles at his daughter.

"They're getting on," Camilla says, as she slips onto a chair beside Jon.

Sniggers from the kitchen drift over to the table, as Jacob and Emma are lost in something their parents are likely too old to find amusing. Jon watches as Emma finishes the last dish and stacks it onto a pile as Jacob empties the water from the sink. Then Jacob leads Emma out of the kitchen and down the hall, and, for the briefest of moments, Jon sees the brush of fingertips and they are gone, out of sight, their presence replaced with the soft beat of music, and the quiet snick of a door being closed. Camilla catches Jon's eye, and he shrugs.

"They met in the store," he says.

"They'll be fine," Camilla says, and sips her coffee. "Jacob is still young, not so experienced."

"He's a good-looking boy."

"Shy in his own way. Like his father."

Bo closes the photo album and slides it to one side. He takes a biscuit and smiles at his wife, then turns to Jon.

"You want to know about the wolf?" he asks.

"Yes. Whatever you can tell me."

"I can show you."

"Bo," Camilla says. "I thought you buried the ewe?"

"I tossed it on the manure pile. Between the pumpkins." He finishes his coffee and stands up. Bo fiddles with a torch by the windowsill as Jon takes his empty mug from the table.

"Let me do that," Camilla says.

She takes the mug from Jon's hand, and glances at her husband. Bo clicks the torch on, tapping the side to steady the beam.

"I threw the halogen lamp at the wolves," he says. "This'll have to do."

The pumpkins are smaller this season, but bright and bold in the torchlight, orange orbs circling a dead sheep. Bo steps onto the manure and drags the sheep by its hind leg to where Jon stands. There is gas in the dead ewe and it seeps out of the stomach, wrinkling Jon's nose as Bo lights the ragged tear in the sheep's leg with torchlight.

"Here," he says, tracing the bite marks with a small twig from the ground.

Jon kneels next to the sheep, presses his face closer to the leg, and holds out his hand for Bo's torch. He focuses the beam on the leg, looking for the tell-tale crushing of bone, but all he sees is a bite.

"What about the belly?"

Bo grasps the sheep's hooves, grunts as he turns it. Jon gags at the smell and then shines the light on the sheep's belly. There is a ring of teeth marks, puncture wounds that fit what he knows of wolves' teeth, but not dissimilar to those of a large dog, such as a German Shepherd, or something similar. The location of the bite is more interesting. He stands up and moves to the neck, playing the torchlight up and down as Bo turns the sheep's head. Jon straightens and takes a step away from the sheep. Bo takes a rag from a rusty nail bent into a wooden post and wipes his hands.

"There's nothing on the neck," Jon says. "The bite on the leg is too light for a wolf."

Bo tosses the rag onto the ground. He stares at Jon.

"But the stomach bite is interesting. A single wolf might grab at the leg, but it wants to get the neck," Jon says, and presses his fingers together like a huge jaw. "It clamps, holds on, suffocating or paralysing the sheep, or deer… If it can bring the animal down, with a good hold around the neck, then, after a time, the prey will stop, it will be suffocated. And the wolf can start to eat there," he says, and points at the stomach. "If there is more than one wolf, after they have run the prey for a time, harrying it with nips at the legs, then one wolf will leap on its back and go for the neck. When it slows, others might go for the stomach, gutting it, and the animal dies from multiple wounds, bleeding out as the wolves eat." Jon shines the torch at the leg. "Wolves have a tremendous crushing power. A sheep's leg is so much thinner than a moose, for example, so I would expect the bone to be broken." He plays the light from the leg to the head of the sheep. "It's inconclusive," he says. "It could be a wolf. It could be a dog. I don't know for sure. If there were more…"

"I've built a fence," Bo says.

"It won't stop the wolf."

Another low whine drifts over the two men, and Jon shines the torch in the direction he thinks he can hear the sound.

"It's a cow," Bo says, and nods towards the farmhouse. "I need to wash my hands."

There is more coffee in a thermos flask on the table, another plate of biscuits. Jon kicks off his shoes as Bo washes his hands, fills two mugs with coffee and then follows Bo down the hall. The soft beat of music thumps through the walls of Jacob's room, and Jon is tempted to check on his daughter. Bo knocks on the door as they pass and says something about biscuits. He leads Jon into the lounge where Camilla is reading.

"They haven't come out?" Bo asks.

"Sounds as though they are enjoying the music," she says, smiling.

Bo slumps into an armchair, the sleeves covering the arms of the chair are worn, and he slips his finger inside the largest of the holes as he tilts his head to look through the door and down the hall. Jon sits next to Camilla on the sofa.

"Did you see the sheep?" she asks.

"Yes."

"And? What do you think?"

"It could be a wolf, or it could be a dog."

"You're not sure?"

"Perhaps if I had seen it when it was fresh."

"Then you need to see more," Bo says, and stands up.

"That would mean more attacks. I don't want to…" Camilla stops speaking as Bo walks across the room, down the hall, and knocks on Jacob's door.

When there is no reply, Bo opens the door slowly, and then pushes it wide as he looks inside the room. Camilla puts down her book as Bo returns to the lounge.

"They're not there," he says.

"What?"

"The window is wide open. They must have gone outside."

"Without saying anything?" Camilla looks at Jon.

Jon takes out his phone dials Emma's number as Camilla uncurls her legs, reaches for her phone on the coffee table, and calls her son. There is no reply to either call, so both Jon and Camilla put their phones onto the coffee table.

Jon lifts his head at another low bestial whine as it slices through Jacob's open window, sharper now, darker, like the night.

"You say that's a cow?"

Bo nods.

Jon laughs and leans back in the sofa. He is no stranger to the howl of a wolf, and it amuses him that now, on the west coast of Denmark, perhaps the tamest countryside in Europe, he can feel the hair prickling on the back of his neck, as he thinks of his daughter, and wonders where she might be, at night, in wolf country.

"It sounds like a dog," Jon says.

"It's a cow. A bullock calling for its mother."

"Bo," Camilla says.

"That's what it is."

"No, Bo, not that. What about Jacob?"

Bo looks at his watch. His picks up his mug of coffee and sits down.

"It's almost midnight," he says. "We'll give him

half an hour."

"It's okay," Jon says. "I'm sure it's not Jacob's fault. Emma can be quite forward, although she thinks I don't know, that I don't see it. It's just as likely she suggested a moonlight walk." Jon taps his leg and looks at Bo. "A bullock?"

Bo shrugs. "Who knows. It's a bit like the sheep, isn't it? It depends on who's looking. It depends on their experience. I hear a bullock. You hear a dog."

"Bo," Camilla says again, with wide eyes and a nod towards their guest.

"Or maybe, you hear a wolf," is Bo's reply to his wife.

Chapter 12

Jacob teases Emma through the fields with tales of werewolves. He laughs as she slaps him on the arm to stop, says nothing, barely breathes, when her fingertips brush his, when her body is so close he feels the heat of her skin. He stops at the hedgerow, points at a low opening through the bramble wall, and whispers something about a Holloway – an ancient path hidden from view. He feels the tips of Emma's shoes as she steps close and snuggles inside his arms. She lifts her head; he feels her breath on his chin, blistering the light hairs on his upper lip, and then her lips… He feels her lips, soft, warm, the sweat from her skin, the tip of her tongue pressing between his lips as their mouths open.

He is lost.

He is back in the store, dazzled by the girl, a deer in the headlights. Her father is the wolf man, she could be a werewolf. She is hunting. He rises, and her fingers brush the very tip of him, and then she steps back, and he breathes. He sweats and swallows as if it might help him breathe evenly, in and out.

"Did you like that?" she whispers.

"Yes."

Emma smiles, takes his hand. It is hot, slippery, like his own.

"What's that?" she asks, and points at the Holloway.

"A secret."

"Like this?" she says and brushes him again with the very tips of her fingers.

"Yes," he says, not sure what to say, what to do.

"Show me." Emma points at the gap between the

brambles.

"You won't tell?"

"Never."

"Not my dad? Not yours?"

"No," she says. She pinches the skin on the back of his hand. The sudden pain shocks him.

"Okay," he says, and leads her through the bramble door.

The thorns scratch and tear, stick in their skin, draw thin trails of blood like leaf veins across their hands. Emma stops, and Jacob untangles her hair that smells of coconut and sweat. It smells of the night. He smoothes a loose strand of hair through his fingers, presses it against her cheek, and tries to kiss her.

"No," she says, eyes shining. "Later."

He swallows again, confused but excited. It is difficult to crawl with the throbbing between his legs. He stoops when and where he can and leads the way along a narrow ditch roofed with brambles. At one point it is possible for them to stand, with their heads bent, and he takes Emma's hand, curls his fingers between hers, and presses one finger to his lips.

"Why?" she breathes.

"You'll see."

The brambles tug at their hair and Jacob pulls Emma down into a crouch, and they crawl another ten metres, sinking lower to the ground until they are flat, and the warm soil spins a heady tang into their noses. Jacob inches closer to Emma, presses his lips against her ear.

"It's a German bunker," he whispers, "from the war. This is the trench."

Emma turns; her lips brush Jacob's cheek as she

moves her mouth to his ear, only to stop at the sound of movement. She freezes, unsure what she is seeing. She glances at Jacob, and he smiles, his teeth just visible in the black tunnel of the bramble trench.

The cub has big ears. Emma can't see the colour of its fur, but its eyes suck at the moon and shine wet and black, as it tumbles in the leaf litter in front of a jagged hole in the thick concrete base of the bunker. More eyes bob out of the hole, until they too soak up the moon and shine. The largest nips the first, and the third tumbles behind it. Jacob squeezes Emma's hand, and extends one long finger, slowly, through the soil, to point at the bushes concealing the northern approach to the bunker.

"I've named her Twiggy," he whispers, when his lips find Emma's ear.

She holds her breath as female adult wolf, the face narrower, eyes closer, lifts her head and extends her neck as the first cub slips free of its siblings and bites at the thick pale fur at her throat. She licks the cub and it tumbles down into the teeth and tangle of the thin legs and clumsy paws of its siblings.

Jacob whispers and points. "That one is Grey. Over there."

A large wolf, similar in height to a German Shepherd, splays its paws and works the muscles of its cinnamon-speckled throat. The cubs tumble across to the male, lick at its chops and bustle about the regurgitated meat that the wolf deposits on the ground. The wolf straightens, nostrils flaring, as it scans the area around the den. Jacob squeezes Emma's hand and tugs her away from the wolves, deeper into the Holloway.

They crawl beneath the brambles for another five

minutes, pausing at the thorny entrance to the field. Jacob sits and Emma curls onto his lap, slips her hands around his neck and kisses his ear.

"Thank you."

She kisses his eyes and he closes them. He smells her skin, warm, baked from the sun, as she kisses his brow. Jacob lifts his chin as Emma arches her neck. He moves his lips across her skin to her mouth, ignoring the thorns needling his thighs, just as she ignores the brambles that are tugging at her hair.

They dawdle on the walk back across the field, the dry earth crumbling, dusting, filling the pores of her shoes, his boots, it clings to their skin. He stops at the edge of the sheep paddock, spins his finger for her to turn in the moonlight and removes a twig from her hair and a leaf that is spider-silked to her back. She dusts soil from his shoulders, smiles, grips his chin, and kisses him. Her hand brushes his shorts and he gasps.

"Don't," he says. "I can't control it."

Emma grins, slips her hand across his groin and skips back.

"Now we have to wait, we can't go in yet," Jacob says.

"Why?"

"*Why?* Just look."

Emma laughs and walks towards the farmhouse.

"Wait."

"What?"

"Remember, don't say a word about the den, dad doesn't know," he says.

"Alright."

"And don't tell your dad either."

Emma nods. She takes Jacob's hand and they

climb over the stile in the fence and walk across the paddock. They pause at the corner of the farm building, as the sound of car engines and muffled voices, drifts across the cobblestones.

"Emma?" Jon says.

"Yes, dad." She lets go of Jacob's hand.

He looks at his watch. "It's one o'clock in the morning."

"I know."

Jon opens the car door, holding it as Emma walks beneath the boughs of the oak and climbs into the passenger seat. She looks at Jacob and he waves.

Jacob waits for Jon and Emma to leave and then looks back towards the farmhouse. His father is sitting on the steps.

"Where've you been?" he asks as Jacob crosses the courtyard.

"We went for a walk."

"Nice for some."

"Yes."

"Your mum was worried."

"I know."

"You do?"

"No," he says, and looks up. "Maybe."

"You like her?"

Jacob nods.

Bo stands up as Jacob reaches for the handle of the door.

"No," Bo says. He grips Jacob's shoulders and turns him towards the rough land behind farmhouse. Jacob slows, and Bo pushes him forwards. "I need your help."

There is an aluminium shed behind a mound of thistled rubble. The grass is dead, wiry beneath the feet, but the nettles and thistles have learned to dig deep, just as Jacob must as they reach the door and his father unlocks the padlock. *We all have our secrets*, he thinks. *And this is my dad's.*

There is a rustle of heavy chain. It stops as the door creaks open, and Jacob steps inside. He freezes at the growls, slavers and snarls. Jacob looks at his father, and Bo nods. There is a thin-handled broom leaning against the wall and Jacob takes it. He holds it like a lance, the brush at the tip, like a shield. Jacob takes a step forwards and the beast growls and lunges, but Jacob is faster – only just. He shoves the brush into the beast's chest, driving it against the back wall as his father grabs the rusted chain, loops it over a wooden spar in the roof and pulls the chain until the beast is stretched at the neck. The growls turn to whispered snarls, and Jacob steps back.

"Food, Jacob," Bo says. "Be quick. I can't hold it forever."

The beast, a large dog, scratches at the rough wooden floor, long claws gouging deep, coiling thick shaves of old wood beneath its paws. Jacob scatters dry food onto the floor of the shed. He tips fetid water into a bowl and then he steps back.

"The broom," Bo says.

Jacob reaches for the broom, looks into the beast's bulging eyes, stares at his constricted neck, and Jacob shakes. He drags the broom across the floor. Places it against the wall. Waits for the nod from his father, and then runs outside. His father lets go of the chain and it bumps over the spar like an anchor tumbling to the bottom of the sea. The beast lunges for the door, and Bo leaps outside, as Jacob flings it shut. The door catches the nose of the beast, until both men can push it closed. There is saliva on the door. It is wet and sticky on Jacob's skin.

"It's done," Bo says, as he nods towards the house. "Come on."

Jacob washes his hands, mumbles good night to his father, and closes the door to his room. Someone has turned off the music. Probably his mother. He purges thoughts of the beast in the shed with long, slow breaths. He takes off his shoes. There is soil on the floor of his room. He should have left his shoes at the door, like his father did.

He turns his head to look out of the window at the sound of someone, or something, blowing through a long pipe, dragging the notes lower and deeper until they are hoarse, coarse whispers. He knows it is the beast. He knows it is a secret.

Eighteen-year-olds are supposed to have secrets, but as far as Jacob knows this is a secret he is not supposed to have; a savage dog chained in the shed at the bottom of the garden. He wonders if the priest imagined such a beast when he suggested his father should get a dog to watch the sheep. Surely the beast is more dangerous than the wolf.

Perhaps that is the point.

Perhaps the beast has a purpose.

Jacob thinks of the wolves, the mother and the cubs. He can't imagine them attacking the sheep. But who will protect the sheep from the beast?

Jacob's phone beeps with a message, and he lifts it from his bedside table. There are two messages from Emma. The second makes his heart leap, and he forgets all about the beast, and calls her number. She answers on the second ring.

"I have to whisper," she says. "Press the phone

to your ear."

He can almost smell her skin, the coconut sweat, the taste of her tongue, the brush of her lips as she tells him what to do, and what she is doing. There is a lump in his throat and he can't swallow, can hardly breathe as he slips his hand inside his shorts, teasing and stroking as Emma guides him with breathy whispers. He imagines he can feel and smell the heat of her body. The sweat of her body. It's musk. It's animal. Wolf like.

"Our secret," she whispers.

"Yes."

"Like the wolves."

"Yes."

Jacob's breath catches in his throat as Emma moans. She begs him to tell her what to do, and he swallows, tongue heavy in his mouth. He whispers something, imagines what she might be doing. The air thickens in the room as the sea is silenced, as the wind changes direction, as the wolf howls.

Wolves are on the wind.

There are wolves among us, there are beasts in the shed, and there are demons in Jacob's head, in his ear, guiding his hand, as he guides hers, and the crickets are silenced, like the sea, as the wolves howl.

Chapter 13

Anton Bjerg leans against the barn door and stares at the burned hulk of the combine harvester parked in the far end of the barn next to the milking shed. He turns on the lights, takes a picture with his phone and sends it to the insurance company. It'll be a week before he hears anything. He walks from the barn to the milking shed. The machines are silent; the stalls empty, the cows are still in the field. He knows he has to bring them in before the heat of the new day makes them and him irritable.

"Maja? Are you in here?"

"Here," she says, and steps out of a stall in the middle of the milking room. "Needed a new cup." She smiles at her husband. "Still thinking about the combine?"

"Yeah," he says. "I just want it out of the way."

"They said it'll be at least a week."

"I know."

"Then stop sulking and go and get the cows." She flicks an oily rag at Anton's bottom as he walks past.

"Don't start something you can't finish," he says, and grins.

"In this heat?"

"Yeah. Autumn, maybe?"

"More like winter. Go on," she says. "I'll be along in a minute."

The track from the milking shed to the pasture winds around a small copse of trees. Anton knows there is an old badger sett in there, and he stops to listen for any indication the badgers might have returned, as he does each morning, before the dawn.

He's read the rewilding books, seen the documentaries, and even cancelled a holiday to attend a conference in the south of England. Maja's not so sure, but he knows she'll come around. Organic is just the first step, and if hadn't been for the drought, they might have had cause to celebrate at the end of the year. But the bank is not convinced. In Anton's experience, they are never convinced, but strangely happy to pump more money into his farm, and others in the area.

The sett is empty.

Anton walks on.

The cows are restless, lowing and braying, snorting, running even. Anton climbs the gate. He looks over the small herd of dairy cattle, just twenty cows and a couple of calves. One of them is lying down at the far end of the field, and the mother is running. Then Anton sees a flash of fur, a creature. It's big, and he leaps down from the gate.

The pasture is dry. Dust clouds burst beneath his boots as he runs, scattering the herd to the side, pressing them against the electric fences. He is almost upon the calf when something races in from his right. It bowls him over and he feels a piercing pain in his muscle at the back of his leg. Anton rolls onto his side, kicking, punching. He tries to get a grip of the throat of the thing that's attacking him, but it shakes him free, snaps at his face, cuts his chin with sharp incisors. Anton shouts, he yells at the thing, and his shouting and yelling stresses the herd, and they charge, wild, confused, frightened across the pasture. He can feel the hooves drumming through the dry earth, and they are upon him. The thing has released his leg, and he curls his knees to his chest, and hides his face behind his elbows until all is black and he can't breathe for dust.

There is a blur as Anton thinks he is flying, levitating at the very least. But if could do such a thing, he would do it smoothly, without all the twisting and turning. And then there is the noise. He might have heard his wife's voice, but, now there is only thunder, and the beating of great wings. A door slides within a groove and slams shut. The beating and roaring recede, and then there is a sharp prick of something in his arm, and the beating, the roaring, the biting, and the drumming are gone.

He sees faces. They are all Maja's face, but the voice is different each time. Anton frowns as one of the Majas has a deep voice, like a man, another light, a third old. It is the fourth Maja, the one who holds his hand and strokes his cheek that is the real Maja and, as he opens his eyes, he sees her, catches one of her tears on his cheek, just below his eye.

"Anton," she says. "You're awake." She waits a moment and says, "Your father's here."

"Where?"

"Here, in hospital." Maja wipes her tear from his cheek. "You're in Skive. You came here by helicopter."

"What happened to it?"

"To what? You were trampled by the cows. You're lucky."

"No," Anton says. "The dog? What happened to it?"

Maja glances at Anton's leg. The hospital staff removed the sheets; he was sweating beneath. The bandage around his lower leg is bloody, it needs replacing.

"You had a rabies shot. You have to have more. I can't remember how many."

"It was a wolf, Anton," Aage says, as he approaches the bed.

Maja lets go of Anton's hand. "I'll be outside," she says.

Anton looks at his father. The spinning and roaring has stopped but everything is still moving too fast. Anton struggles to remember when he last spoke to his father.

"It was before your wedding," Aage says. "I gave you my blessing."

"I didn't want it."

"I know."

Anton tries to move, but his chest is wrapped tight, bound to the bed.

"Your ribs are a mess."

"I can't feel them."

"Then the morphine is working."

"Why are you here?"

Aage pulls a chair up to the bed and sits down.

"My son is in hospital, badly wounded after a wolf attack. I had to see you."

"It was a dog."

"No, son." Aage shakes your head. He points at the drip plugged into Anton's arm. "Too much morphine," he says.

Maybe he's right, Anton thinks. He remembers teeth, fur at the neck. It was fast, big; it pushed him to the ground. It ran away before the stampede. It could have been a wolf.

"Bo's sheep was attacked. There are wolves in the area. Your cattle are lucky you came when you did. Not so lucky for you. But you only lost one calf. The vet is looking at it. The police were called."

"The police?"

"They arrived just minutes before the helicopter. Maja had to clear the field. You couldn't be moved. Bo was there. He helped moved the cattle, together with his son. You know Jacob?"

"Yes, of course."

"They didn't want the helicopter to spook the cows. But they had to move you quickly…"

"You said the vet was there. You mean Viktoria?"

Aage nods. "She came to look at the cow. Jon Østergård, the wolf man, he was there too. It's been on the television. The first wolf attack on a human in Denmark."

"It was a dog."

Aage takes his son's hand. "It was a wolf," he says, and nods at the drip.

Anton looks at his father's hand, sees a wet sheen film his eyes. It has been so long since his father took his hand. So long since they last talked – really talked.

"What does Viktoria say?"

"She says it's a wolf."

"And Jon?"

Aage takes a deep breath. He pats Anton's hand and stands up. Anton tries to follow him around the room, but his father's pacing forces him to close his eyes. The room spins of its own accord. The addition of a pirouetting priest is too much.

"Aage?"

"Yes?"

"Stop moving," Anton says.

"Alright."

"You were telling me about Jon."

"He wants to see your leg."

"That's fine. He's welcome to look."

"I think it is better if he doesn't." Aage rests his hands on the rail at the end of the bed. "Anton, the media is pouncing on this. It changes the debate. Lærke Wang, the journalist from *Danmarks Radio*, is going from house to house. Tilde Sørensen has been commissioned to write about the Thyrup wolf for *Politiken*. Membership is soaring in the Society."

"What society?"

"For a wolf-free Denmark. They are considering renting premises in Ringkøbing. Don't you see?" The bed trembles and Aage's knuckles turn white. "Popular opinion is gaining ground. Thyrup is on the map and Christiansborg is listening. If the wolf hadn't attacked you…"

"It was a dog."

"A dog? Come on, Anton. You're an intelligent man. A dog couldn't do that, and a dog attack would never demand a helicopter, three police cars, two television crews and more journalists than Thyrup has ever seen. It was a wolf that attacked you." Aage stabs a finger at the door. "Maja understands."

"Understands *what*?"

"That the community is suffering. That people are scared, and now, a strong man has been nearly killed by a wolf…"

"The cows."

"Yes, the cows, startled by the wolf that savaged your leg." Anton," Aage says, as he sits down. "Thyrup needs your help. Tell them from your heart what you know to be true. Tell them about the wolf. Please, Anton. It's important. Now more than ever."

My father is begging, Anton thinks. He has never seen him beg, never seen him so animated. From his castle on the hill, his church, Aage has watched over his flock, seen the numbers of his congregation dwindle, when Sunday sermons for many became confirmations, weddings, funerals, perhaps three to four visits a year. Yes, there are wolves In Thyrup, Anton believes that. And when the wolves came, the church became a beacon. It had the words to console, chapter and verse to protect, psalms to strengthen. Aage has become a shepherd and his flock need him, at the church, in the community. If they see the old priest walking in the woods, they will walk with him, without fear, protected by God. The Devil's hounds would not dare to strike a man of the cloth.

And they didn't.

They struck his son instead.

Perhaps, Anton thinks.

Aage wipes his brow and turns on the television.

"The news," he says. "Your story is headlining."

Anton watches the news article, seeing the helicopter lifting off from his pasture, the police, his neighbours. He sees Camilla there, holding Maja's hand. Cameras are flashing in a corner of the field, and the video is cut with the image of Viktoria and Jon examining the calf. Viktoria declines to comment, but Jon is not so lucky. He seems inexperienced, he is not used to the press. A microphone is shoved towards his face, and Aage turns up the volume.

"You don't think it was a wolf?" Lærke asks.

"I think it could have been a large dog, it may have been a wolf. I cannot say for sure."

"But the veterinarian thinks it is a wolf?"

"You would have to ask her."

"So, you disagree with her findings?"

"I didn't say that."

"But you don't agree."

"No." Jon shakes his head. "I don't. Not before…"

Aage turns the volume down and looks at his son.

"You see? Thyrup needs you. You must say what you saw. Tell them the truth and they will believe you." Aage sighs. "Honestly, Anton, what else could it have been?"

Aage slips the remote into Anton's hand before he leaves. Anton turns up the volume as the Prime Minister is asked for comment.

"I think we need to look closely at the situation, and, in the meantime, recognise and applaud the fantastic job of the doctors, paramedics, nurses and the pilots involved in the tragic accident that occurred in Thorup today."

"*Thyrup*," the journalist says.

"Exactly."

"And what about the wolves?"

"In Thyrup?"

Anton turns up the volume as the Prime Minister pauses at the top of the stairs of the parliament building.

"It's no secret there are wolves in Thyrup."

"Is that something the government will look closely at too?"

"Yes," the Prime Minister says. "Very closely."

Chapter 14

It's too hot on the beach, too hot in her room, too hot downstairs where her father broods, shuffling back and forth across the sand-soaked mats in the kitchen and living room. Emma has never seen him like this, out of his depth, stressed, insecure. She thinks it is the wolves, but the image of the cubs outside the den, the father bringing food, and the mother resting, when she thinks of them it is hard to imagine that they can cause so much trouble. She slips her feet over the side of the bed and grabs her phone.

Jon is staring through the salt-streaked window of the beach house when she walks into the tiny kitchen.

"Dad?"

"I'm alright," he says. "Just making coffee." Jon smiles at his daughter. "Do you want one?"

"It's too hot."

"You can always go and get a coke. A beer if you want."

"We can share a beer."

The first time they shared a beer was the last time. It was hot then too. A beach café on the island of Corfu in Greece. Emma was fifteen, but her dad said she looked like she was twenty-one. The waiters thought so too. Her mum was there. They ate ham and cheese toasties. The meat was sweet. The waiters were dark and mysterious. Their cigarette smoke was richer than anything people smoked in Denmark. The beach was white, the sand warm beneath her feet. Her dad ordered three beers, and, as she took that first illicit sip, her mum and dad told her they were getting a divorce. The holiday was already booked, they said. They couldn't get a refund. They didn't want to ruin it, but that's just what they did and the beer soured in her mouth. Her father finished it for her.

Jon is quiet and Emma knows he is thinking about that beer in Greece. She wonders if she should tell him about the wolves, about the den, if that would change anything. And then she thinks of Jacob and knows that it would change *everything* and she doesn't want that. He might be a summer fling, but right now it's difficult to know.

When Jon carries his coffee into the living area she follows, sits with him at the tiny table. His phone beeps and he takes it out of his pocket, turns it face down on the table.

"That's *Danmarks Radio*. They want to do an interview." Jon sighs. "I don't know what to say."

"Mum would know," Emma says.

"I can't get her involved."

"She doesn't have to get involved, but she could tell you what to say." Emma frowns. "You don't know what she does, do you?"

"Of course, I do. She works for the Spanish government."

"In the media department, dad," Emma says. "She's not just a wildlife biologist anymore; she deals with the press and stuff. About all kinds of things, including wolves."

Jon checks his watch. "It's early afternoon."

"It's the same time zone, dad." Emma laughs, stands up, and kisses her father on the forehead. "I'm going out for a coke. Stop brooding, call mum, and figure it out. I'll be back in an hour."

"Emma," Jon says, as she slips her sandals on at the door.

"Yes."

"Just an hour, okay? Either that or give me a call."

"Okay."

Since the attack on Anton Bjerg, Thyrup's main street, narrow as it is, has been transformed into a carnival. There are large vans with big, round satellite dishes on the roofs. Journalists blight the pavements with microphones and clusters of cameras. *They are like sharks*, Emma thinks, circling, frenzied, with a scurry of activity at the first scent of a new development, a new angle, or a new witness. It won't be long before they discover where her father is hiding. Emma is surprised they haven't already found him. Then she sees who they have pinholed and she slows to listen to Olivia and Sebastian, as they claim Anton could never have been attacked by a wolf, because they know where the wolves are.

"The wolves were all in the den when he was attacked," Olivia says. "So whatever Anton is saying, whatever the vet is saying, it's all lies."

The crowd murmurs and Emma wonders if Olivia and Sebastian really do know where the den is.

"A man was nearly killed," Lærke says, thrusting the microphone towards Olivia.

Olivia tugs the microphone from the reporter's hand, and steps closer to the camera.

"Wolves are scared of humans, and with good reason. The people of Thyrup have created a monster, where none can be found. What happened yesterday is the result of fear-mongering and ignorance. It is tragic, a man has been hurt – a good man who believes in the diversity of nature, but he has been corrupted by the church – like everyone else in this tiny village," she says, pointing at the church spire, just visible in the distance.

Tourists gathered around the interview shrink as the locals in the crowd jeer and shout, jostling shoulders, adding to the carnival atmosphere. Lærke reaches for the microphone, but Olivia yanks it out of her grasp when she sees Emma in the crowd.

"She knows the truth," Olivia says, pointing. "Her and her father."

Emma's skin itches as the crowd turns. Her feet are lead, refusing to move. The reporter finally wrestles the microphone out of Olivia's hands, and looks at Emma. With a nod to the camera operator, she parts the crowd with the microphone – it's like a wand, crackling with media magic, bursting with energy. With that wand Lærke can curry favour, influence change, create demons and slay monsters. It is magic of the most powerful kind, and it has bewitched Emma. Her sandals have sprouted roots, and they twist through the paving to the bedrock below the village. She cannot move.

"Emma Østergård?" Lærke asks.

"Yes."

"Your father is Jon Østergård?"

Emma looks at the microphone, and Lærke lowers it. The camera operator and the man with the fluffy microphone on the end of a long stick retreat to the van at a nod from the reporter. Emma is alone with Lærke and the crowd. Olivia and Sebastian are busy with a journalist. Emma nods.

"Yes, he's my dad," she says, and looks at the people edging closer.

The tourists among them are easy to spot, their faces bemused, eyes bright. It is the darker looks that unnerve Emma, as the locals, some of whom she remembers seeing at the town meeting, draw closer, pushing past the tourists. They are within a long arm's length, but then Lærke rescues Emma with a light touch of her elbow and a nod to the studio café across the street.

"How about a coffee, Emma," she says. Emma lets Lærke guide her across the street, snapping the roots from beneath her sandals, freeing her feet.

There is a table for two on a small landing at the top of the studio stairs. Emma sits on one side. She can see the sea through the round panes of glass, and the sea breeze blowing through the window lifts the strands of her hair, tickling her cheeks. The breeze dries the sweat beading her brow, and she listens as the reporter's shoes creak upon the wooden stairs.

"I love places like this," Lærke says, as she sits down. The waitress, an artist, brings them coffee and thick-crusted strawberry cake.

When the waitress moves away, Emma asks if this is on the record.

"What?"

"This is an interview," she says. "Am I on the record?"

"This isn't an interview, Emma. It can be if you want it to be. But right now," she says, with a nod to the crowds ambling between the television vans on the street, "this is coffee and cake." Lærke smiles as she sticks the fork into the strawberry, nestled in the vanilla cream. "I love strawberries."

Emma smiles. She is just about to pick up her fork when she remembers her father. Lærke watches her as she sends a quick message. There's no response, and she hopes it means her father is talking on the phone. The irony of talking with the very woman he was trying to avoid flushes into her cheeks.

"Are you alright?"

"Yes," Emma says, and pushes the phone to one side. "Just texting my dad."

"How old are you?"

"Nineteen."

"And how do you like the west coast?"

How do I like the west coast? she wonders. She won't talk about the den of wolves. She won't mention Jacob. She doesn't want to think about the people at the town meeting. What else is there to say?

"There's a lot going on," she says.

"More than Copenhagen?"

"Different. More intense."

"I grew up in Ringkøbing," Lærke says. "It's a lot like this, just a bit bigger." She works on the cake crust with her fork. "Everybody knows everybody over here. So, when something happens to someone, it happens to them all. More or less. It's difficult to understand when you are on the outside. Like your father, for example."

"He's struggling," Emma says, wondering if she should say anything at all.

"I'm not surprised. Besides, he's used to working in the field, with wolves, and now he's working with people."

"He's not good with people, not like this."

"Who is?" Lærke says, and winks.

"We met this man in Alaska," Emma says, "just before we came here. He was a bit weird. Really intense. I think he was an Eskimo." Emma shrugs, as Lærke leans back in her seat. "He said something about the Middle Ages, how the wolf takes people back – their way of thinking – and how they look at the wolf…"

"How they *look* at it?"

"Something about projecting their sins on the wolf. If they punish it or kill it, then they cleanse themselves? I don't know," she says. "It was something he said."

"What do you think? About wolves?"

Before Jacob, the bramble tunnel, and the den, Emma's wolves were the ones in her father's slides. They were a part of him, connected to him, even more than her mother. Their house was full of wolf books. Now their apartment is full of wolf books. Her father complains about having to buy for a second time the books her mother took to Spain. Her mother curses her father when she can't find a book he has in Copenhagen. It is always the same books. They both buy books multiple times, each blaming the other for the empty space on the bookshelf, only to find the book they want beneath a newspaper, or in the car, usually after they have bought a new copy. Then there are the boxes of tapes, the *howling sessions* her father calls them. Emma used to listen to them as a child, curled up in the blankets between her parents. She listened to the wolves while her parents dissected, discussed and disagreed with the meaning. The howling sessions became heated, and Emma withdrew to her room, swapping wolf howls for pop music, wolf picture books for social media, parents for friends, and the wolf loped away from her, until now.

Since Jacob and the den, with bramble cuts on her skin, thorns in her shoes, sand between her toes, wild thoughts in her head, and a heady, unstoppable fire in her chest, the wolf was more real than ever.

Now that she thinks about it, the wolf's ability to inflame and incense, to drive people mad. It wasn't so difficult to imagine anymore.

Lærke sips her coffee, and Emma remembers her question.

"Wolves," she says, "are wild."

"But would you agree that they are a problem?"

"Only to people."

Lærke reaches into her bag and places a small digital recorder on the table. She catches Emma's eye, slides her finger over the power button.

"When I'm not in front of the camera, I also blog for DR," she says. "Can I interview you? On the record?"

"What does that mean, exactly?"

"It means I can quote what you say and write your name beside it."

"I'm only nineteen."

"You're an adult."

"I don't know."

The straw weave of the seat starts to scratch her skin, and Emma flushes again at the thought of not listening to her own advice, wondering how she ended up in an interview. And then she sees her father, striding up the road from the beach house, and smiles. He got the text and this is his answer.

Chapter 15

The warm wind is better than air conditioning. Emma props her bare feet out of the window as Jon drives north along the coast, away from Thyrup. Emma's memories of the studio café are hours old, forgettable, until her father teases her about giving advice, and not taking it.

"You weren't there," she says. "I was ambushed. The crowd was getting ugly."

"Ugly?" Jon laughs. "Dad, dad, the crowd is getting *ugly*."

"It's not funny dad."

"It is a little," he says, and then he remembers the town meeting, and suddenly it's not funny at all. "Emma, I've been thinking."

"What about?"

"Do you want to go home?"

"Copenhagen?"

"Yes."

She's quiet for a moment, puzzling the question, not sure about her answer.

"Alone?"

"I have to stay here. At least for another few weeks. I had a call from Christiansborg while you were out. They need some answers, and, to be honest, Emma, I don't know where to start."

"Did you call mum?"

"Yes," he says. "I mean, she was helpful, in her own way, but…"

"She didn't have time."

"No."

"Story of *her* life," Emma says, as she thinks of the times when she has to drop everything to talk to her mum – her terms, her time. "What about that man in Alaska? The Eskimo. Can't you call him?"

"I was thinking about it."

"Do it," she says, and opens the Internet browser on her phone. "Right now, it's six-thirty here, and eight-thirty in the morning in Alaska."

"Right," Jon says. He slows as they approach a village. "So what do you think? About going home?"

"I'll stay."

"You're sure?"

"If you want me around."

"I like having you *around*," Jon says. "I just get a little nervous when there are boys involved."

"That's my business, dad."

"Sure," he says and then slows as they pass a local supermarket. He flicks the indicator, slows up and parks on the opposite side of the street."

"I thought we were going out for dinner?"

"We are. There's just…" Jon shields his eyes from the glare of the sun and squints at a man carrying a large bag out of the store. "That's dog food," he says.

"What?"

"Bo. He's at the store. He's buying dog food. I didn't know he had a dog. Has Jacob said anything about a dog?"

"I'm not a spy, dad."

"I know, but…"

"No, I'm pretty sure they don't have a dog."

"Alright," Jon says, and pulls away from the curb.

They pass two more villages before Jon asks Emma to use her phone to find the restaurant.

"It was supposed to be a surprise," he says. "The only vegetarian restaurant on the west coast, probably."

"I eat meat, dad. I had meatballs the other night."

"You said you were vegetarian on the drive over."

"I was angry," she says, throwing a twist of exasperation into her voice. *It isn't hard*, she thinks, her father has *exasperating* down to a fine art.

Emma searches for the restaurant and taps into the Google Maps app on her phone. There is another twelve kilometres, a straight road with sand dunes and campsites on the left-hand side, parched fields on the right. Jon follows the verbal directions from Emma's phone. Emma scans the fields. She pulls her feet from the window, sits up and slaps the dashboard.

"Stop," she says.

"What is it?"

"Stop now."

Jon checks the mirror, slows to let a car pass, and then stops on the side of the road.

Emma is quiet, concentrating. Then she points. "There. A wolf."

It's as if Jon doesn't believe there are wolves in his backyard, in his own country. Maybe he doesn't know where to look. He feels as though the people of Thyrup, with all their *wolf-mongering*, have stripped him of his field skills. But those same people have ignited something in his daughter, and she points and guides him to the slow lope of the wolf across the stubble and dust of the corn field. The wolf stops, lifts its head, as if it smells something. And then Jon sees it. A small car parked in the entrance to the field. The window is open and there is something long and thin, black against the silver panels, poking out of the window.

"Emma, look," Jon says, as he puts the car in gear.

She sees the car, stretches across her dad to slam her hand on the horn, as she shouts out of the window for the wolf to run.

"Why doesn't he run?"

The wolf turns between the twists of corn. Emma holds her breath as the wolf looks right through her. Her hand slips from the horn, and she gasps as the car jerks forward, making her seatbelt tighten.

"Dad?"

"Hold on," he says.

There is a withered hedge at the entrance to the field. Jon accelerates along the road, yanks the wheel down to the right and spins into the field.

"It's still there," Emma says, as she grasps the dashboard.

"And so is he," Jon says, as he bumps the car over the furrows.

There is a passenger in the car, pointing at them. The rifle – they can see it clearly now – slides further out of the window. The tracks of the combine harvester are deep, running parallel to the road. Jon grips the steering wheel as he bumps the Toyota between the hard-crested waves of earth, accelerating over the troughs, and peppering the underside of the car with pebbles, small rocks, clods of dried earth. Emma presses her hand against the ceiling, fumbles her fingers through the handle above the door.

"Emma?"

"I'm alright," she shouts. "Keep going."

There is a shot, and the wolf stands, trots a few paces, as the silver car rolls forwards. The rifle slips at an angle, wedged between the seat and the door as the driver chases the wolf.

Jon closes the gap between them and the silver car, another Toyota, to within ten metres. He swerves into the tracks of the combine, dipping Emma into the trough and closer to the field, as the wheels on the driver's side churn at the crest of the harvester's track.

"Dad," she screams, as the driver lifts the rifle and points it at their car. It is pointing right at Emma.

Jon shifts down a gear, stamps on the accelerator pedal, and curses the Toyota out of the combine tracks and into a collision course with the silver car. Emma closes her eyes as Jon slams the front of the Toyota into the smaller car, spinning them away from the wolf, and into the next field. The passenger, a woman, older than Jon, gives them the finger, while the driver accelerates out of the field and onto a small road. The bumper hangs at an angle, grinding along the surface of the asphalt until the car is gone, hidden by a row of trees.

Jon stops the car. The engine stalls as he lifts his feet from the pedals.

"Are you okay?" he asks.

"I'm okay."

"Good," he says. Jon opens the door. Removes his belt and vomits into the field.

The wolf is gone.

Emma takes her father's hand as they walk through the field, searching for the spot where the wolf lay. Jon finds the hair, the last twist of winter fur, pinched between the thick dry stalks. He teases it between his fingers and scans the field, as Emma finds another clump of fur.

"Dad," she says, as she stands up. "What did we

just do?"

"I really don't know."

"Do you think they were going to shoot it?"

"Yes."

"It's against the law."

"Yes," he says, and hikes a thumb at their car. "I'm not sure what we did was completely legal either."

"Did you see the woman? She was mum's age. It's crazy what wolves make people do."

"Maybe people are just crazy, wolf or no wolf."

The sun is lower now, and Emma says she is too excited to eat. They walk back to the car. The police pull them over at the next village and one of the officers asks Emma what happened, and while she explains, the other inspects scratches and dents in the bumper, the corn clamped between the panels and the pebble strikes on the hubcaps and wheel arches.

"This could be expensive," the officer says.

"I was stupid," Jon says. "But they had a rifle. They shot at the wolf. What else could I do?"

"Whatever they did, you endangered their lives and your own, and the life of your daughter. It wasn't smart. You were lucky, but it's a huge price to pay for a wild animal. Are four human lives worth one wolf? Is it worth your daughter's life?"

"Excuse me," Jon says.

He takes two steps and retches onto the road. Emma jogs around the car, but he waves her away. They don't talk on the way back to the beach house, passing through the neighbouring villages, seeing silver cars at every crossroads, in every drive, behind every tree. Jon stops at the store and Emma follows him inside. She hears a woman's voice and realises she hasn't checked her phone – Google is still trying to guide them to the vegetarian restaurant. She starts to giggle.

"Emma?"

Emma turns the screen towards her father, gives him the phone and puts a bag of frozen meatballs and a tub of potato salad into the basket. *Half vegetarian*, she thinks, and carries their dinner to the car as Jon pays at the register.

They don't recognise the car parked in one of the two spots reserved for the beach house. Jon parks next to it. Only when they reach the house do they realise they have a visitor. Aage Dahl is standing by their front door, a cigarette in his hand.

"I hope you don't mind," he says, as Jon unlocks the door. "I've just come from the hospital. I thought you might like to know about Anton?"

"Maybe tomorrow," Jon says. "It's been a long night."

"Just five minutes?"

Jon stands to one side as Emma walks into the house. She kicks off her sandals.

"Not tonight," Jon says, and closes the door.

The sun projects the priest's shadow up the path as he walks to his car. Emma watches him. She waits until he is gone, and then joins her father at the table.

"You sent him away."

"Yes."

"Why did he just turn up? He could have called."

"That's his way." He beckons to Emma. "Wolf fur," he says, as he plucks a tuft of winter fur from the top of her pocket.

"I put it there," she says.

"I know." Jon presses the fur to his nose, twists it

between his fingers. "Whatever happens tomorrow," he says, "I want you to think about going back to Copenhagen."

"I'm not leaving. Especially not now."

"It's getting out of control, Emma. Things like this aren't meant to happen."

"I think they happen all the time dad, in wolf country. You should call that man, the Eskimo. I bet he would tell you. It's probably worse in America – everyone has guns."

Jon nods and walks into the kitchen. The sun sets as the meatballs warm in the oven. It wasn't quite the evening he had imagined, and thoughts of wolf madness prick at his conscience. He looks at Emma, curled on the sofa, her phone in her lap. It beeps, but she ignores it. *How could he risk her life like that?* The thought, the memory, twists his gut. Jon leans against the counter, presses his hand to his face, feels the tears well in the creases of his palm.

"It's too much, Emma," he says. He watches her pad across the floor, tears dripping down his cheek and into her hair as she curls her arms around him.

"It's okay, dad. You're going to be okay. I won't let anything happen to you."

"No?" he says and strokes her hair.

"Actually," she says, "I think it's going to be easier now. You're starting to fit in."

"How's that?"

"Everyone around here is wolf sick. You're practically a local."

Chapter 16

The gull on the roof of the beach house wakes Jon as it picks at the thatched roof. He dresses, yawning as he fiddles with the buttons of his shirt. The table is laid for breakfast and Jon finds Emma's note tucked between the box of cereal and the cafetière of fresh coffee. He reads the note tucks it into his pocket and tries not to think of what his daughter might be doing with the farmer's son so early in the morning. Jon pours a cup of coffee and glances out of the window as the shadow of the gull flashes past the window.

Jon takes a long time to walk to the car, dropping the rubbish from the kitchen into the wheelie bin on his way. Then he checks the post-box, looks for the gull, considers walking onto the beach to look at the sea, anything to avoid looking at the scratches and dents on the Toyota, the strands of corn wedged into the cracks in the panel. As he walks around the car he realises it's not as bad as he feared. He finds a note under the windscreen wiper, the priest's handwriting is a scrawl of black upon a damp piece of paper torn from a notebook, the mobile number is bold, black, the ink blurring ever so slightly at the edges. The heat of the day has yet to strike the beach, and the dew, this close to the coast, has a salty sheen.

The car starts without a problem, and Jon sighs, thankful for the small things all of a sudden. He drives through the village and takes the road to the Falk farm, turning onto the beach-lined gravel road a few kilometres outside of Thyrup. Camilla is in the courtyard, waving her hands at someone Jon cannot see, but he recognises Olivia and her friend, Sebastian, as he parks his car beside Bo's tractor.

Camilla's voice is sharp, the words blunt, threatening, they jab and cut across the courtyard, as Jon gets out of the car and walks towards her.

"You're not welcome here," she says to the couple and points at the road. "I want you to leave."

"We're not leaving before we talk to your husband," Olivia says.

"He's not here."

"We'll wait."

"Then I'll call the police. This is private property. You have to leave." Camilla's shoulders sag as she sees Jon. The hard lines on her face soften as she catches his eye.

"I think it's best if you go," Jon says, as he walks around Olivia to stand beside Camilla.

"You're taking her side?" Olivia says.

"I'm not on any sides," he says. "But Camilla doesn't want you here. You're trespassing."

Olivia stares at Jon, her eyes blue steel in a white face, her skin taut. "You need to decide who you are protecting, them or the wolf." She nods at Sebastian and they leave, dead leaves swirling at their feet as a warm breath of wind curls around the base of the oak tree.

"They just wouldn't leave," Camilla says, watching as Olivia leads Sebastian across the field to the left of the gravel road, bending and flattening a path through the corn all the way to the main road. "She wouldn't say what they wanted either. But I know," she says. "Those damned wolves. I'm sorry, Jon. I just wish they weren't here. There has been trouble of one kind or another ever since they came."

"I'm beginning to understand," he says.

Camilla frowns as she looks across the courtyard.

"What happened to your car?"

"An accident. My fault."

"Are you hurt?"

"No."

"Emma?"

"She's alright," he says, hairs prickling on his arms as he remembers what he did, how he put Emma's life in danger, because of the wolf. "Can we go inside?" he says.

It's early, but the farmhouse has a mid-morning quiet about it, as if the occupants have been awake for half the day already. Jon realises they probably have. Camilla makes fresh coffee as Jon looks at the old photo of the farm. He squints at the triangle of rough ground behind the farmhouse and looks out of the window by the dining table. He can just see an aluminium shed behind the rubble and thistles; the shed is at least as old as the photograph.

Camilla warms a handful of bread rolls in the oven and places them in a basket next to their coffee on the table. She cuts and butters them as Jon sits down.

"What did you want to talk about?" she asks.

"I don't know," he says. "I thought Emma might be here. She left early this morning, before breakfast."

"That's Jacob's fault. He took off before sunrise on his moped, with a bag of rolls, jam and coffee." Camilla smiles. "I always wondered what he would be like, when he fell in love. This is his first time. He's smitten with your daughter."

"I know," Jon says.

"And you're worried?"

"Not about Jacob. It's me I'm worried about. How should I act? What should I do? Should I be nervous?"

"About Jacob?" Camilla sits down. "He might have the surfer look, but he rarely goes to the beach. He's too busy trying to be his father, although that doesn't always work out. Bo is an intense man. Jacob is softer than he is. I'm not sure he has what it takes to be a farmer, not that he has much choice." Jon waits as Camilla finds a pot of jam from the cupboard. "Strawberry," she says. "About the only thing growing this year."

"Why doesn't he have a choice?"

"Bo can't and won't sell Falk Farm. We owe millions of kroner. He's already half a million in debt from this year alone. But it's next year he worries about. Once Jacob is finished with Gymnasium, he will work here on the farm. He'll die here too." Camilla squeezes Jon's hand. "You don't have to worry about Emma, she doesn't strike me as the farming type. But maybe, if it doesn't cause you too much worry, we could just let them enjoy the last of the summer. Let him fall in love. When she breaks his heart, his dad will keep him busy. He'll be fine."

"You think she'll do that? Break his heart?"

"Jon," Camilla says. There is a light in her eyes that lifts the corners of her mouth. "You know she will. Even if she doesn't want to, or intend to, she's a beautiful young lady. She's a city girl, different to the girls here in the village and at the Gymnasium. He's known *them* all his life. He was lost the moment he saw her. But I'm glad, Jon, really. Glad that he gets to experience love at this age, before the worry of the farm sets in and eats away at him, like it does his father."

Jon looks out of the window at the shed as the

wind picks up and lifts the edge of the door. The hinges creak and he sees a movement, it's the corner of a white plastic bag that is trapped between the shed door and the frame.

"They'll be back soon," Camilla says. "I think he wanted to take her to the dunes. There's a bunker on the beach. It's one of the bigger ones. When the tide is out you can crawl inside, all the way in, and climb a ladder up to the roof. Bo and I used to go there when we were their age. That's where they'll be. I'm sure of it."

"And Bo is in the field?"

"The one furthest from the house." Camilla points. "There, you can just see a black beech tree, no leaves. It was struck by lightning a few years ago. The trunk is split in two. You'll find him there if you want to talk to him."

Jon walks around the back of the farmhouse. There is a gap between the trees and bushes dividing the fields and the rough ground around the farmhouse. He stops at the shed, peers inside, and tugs the white bag away from the door. It is the same bag he saw Bo carry out of the shop the day before. There is a handful of dry pellets on the floor of the shed. Jon cups his hand over his nose and steps inside, bumps his head on the chain hanging from a wooden spar in the roof. He tosses the bag inside the shed and closes the door. He slides the bolt into place, pinches his finger, and sucks at a drop of blood at the tip.

It is not difficult to find Bo. The dust and gulls following the combine harvester rise high above the trees between the fields. Another man is driving the tractor and trailer beside the harvester. Jon recognises him from Wednesday's meeting. He finds Bo standing beside a newer tractor with a large, square plastic tank on the back.

"I'm on fire watch," he says, as Jon picks his way across the stubble of corn.

"But this is your field?"

"My field, his crop," Bo says, and points to the man driving the harvester. "I'll earn more from renting it out to him than he will this year." Bo shrugs. "That's one thing I did right. But," he says, and kicks at the earth. "I won't take his money. I can't afford to. I'll need his help next year."

Bo points at the parched pastures closer to his farm. The sheep are lying down, inside the partially finished fence.

"I lost two more to the heat. I can't get them to drink. The ewes are drying up, and the lambs are getting weak. I was going to keep them, but they're too small. If I slaughter them now, I might have enough money to feed the rest next year, but it's going to be tight. If the wolves take one more, they might as well take them all. Of course, if the bloody politicians would just pay compensation for the dead sheep."

"Have you thought about getting a dog?"

A pocket of wind drifts across the field, pressing corn dust and parched earth into the folds of Jon's shirt. He spits dust from his mouth as Bo stares at him. The dust curls away and into the hedgerow, coating the leaves with a film of silt.

"I don't need a dog," he says. "I have a fence."

"Fences are expensive," Jon says. "A dog would be…"

"More work. I don't need any more animals on

this bloody farm. Not another mouth to feed. Anyway, a dog would just be one more thing for the wolves to kill." Bo spits. "That's right, isn't it?"

"Wolves have killed dogs in America."

"I know," Bo says. "I did a search on the Internet after the meeting. Wolves killed a whole village of dogs in Alaska, one winter."

"I read that too."

"The biologists – like you – said it was a bad winter, but they couldn't explain why the wolves didn't eat the dogs. They just left the bodies."

"I can't explain it."

Bo stares at Jon. "I think they just don't like dogs," he says.

"That's one explanation."

The thrashing of the harvester blades slows, and the field is silent as the farmers take a short break to move a couple of large rocks. The quiet is punctuated by two dull cracks of rocks being tossed into the crate of ballast at the front of the tractor.

"You know," Bo says, "I still haven't figured you out. You're a wolf biologist, but you don't have any answers. You're just as much in the dark as we are."

"I am," Jon says.

"Why?"

Jon lets his focus drift across the field. In his mind he doesn't see the trees, instead he sees a thick blanket of snow with wolves in the distance – his Arctic wolves. The ice beads in the fur around their muzzles, snow drifts through the thick white fur, clumping and balling between the pads of their huge paws. The male, Gere, lifts his paw to bite at the balls of ice. Freke waits for him, slitting her eyes and dipping her nose as loose snow scratches across the barren ground, between boulders of granite blistered with black lichen. Gere trots to her side, licks at her muzzle and breaks into a run, teasing in one direction, darting in another. Jon was there. He described it in lengthy passages of tightly-spaced notations, his notepad pressed against his thigh as Inuk, his Greenlandic guide, boiled water for their tea. That was the night Gere bit at Jon's ankles as he pissed in the snow. He smiles at the memory, and the snow melts and the field drifts back into focus, just as the farmer climbs back into the cab of the combine harvester.

"Why don't I have any answers?" Jon brushes the dust from his shirt. "I thought I did. I *do* know wolves, but not these wolves. *These* wolves are surrounded by people." Jon looks at Bo. "People are my problem."

Chapter 17

Jacob says they could look for amber, or maybe even swim. No-one is around, and Emma strips to the bikini she wears beneath her shorts and t-shirt. Jacob roars his way through the waves, lifting his arms as the surf crashes against his body. Emma shrieks as she runs past him, diving into the water as soon as it is deep enough. She bursts to the surface, giggling and spluttering. She gasps at the cold as her body settles, acclimatises, and she slips beneath the waves, smoothes her hair against her head, and kicks her feet, just enough to keep her head above the water, her eyes on Jacob as he swims towards her. When he is close, when their bodies touch, his eyes widen, and she curls her bikini top around his neck. The waves lift them as they kiss. She runs her fingers through his hair. He cups a trembling hand around her breast. The surf carries them to the beach, and they kiss in the sand gasping as the sea surges, catching them unawares. Emma giggles as Jacob struggles to his feet. She points at his shorts, and he blames her. She takes his hand.

"Where's my bikini?"

He doesn't know. The surf has taken it.

"You're beautiful," he says.

Emma squeezes his hand, and they bump gritty, salty shoulders as they walk to the bunker, crawl inside, coat their bodies in a layer of fine white sand, and climb to the roof.

"My mum used to bring my dad here," Jacob says, as they lie on a sandy blanket, head towards the dunes, feet pointing to the sea, toes touching. "When they were courting."

"Courting?"

"Yeah, you know…"

She giggles. "*Courting.* It sounds old."

"They are, I suppose."

Emma creases her brow and purses her lips. "Are you *courting* me, Jacob Falk?"

"Are you asking?"

"I am, because if you are…" She laughs, twitches as he tickles her. "*If* you are…"

"Then you'll have to tell your father?"

Jacob smoothes his hand along her cheek, brushes wet hair from her eyes, and kisses her. He opens his eyes as she nibbles at his bottom lip, and he pulls back.

"What?" she whispers.

"I don't know how to do that," he says. "The biting. I don't know that kind of thing."

Emma smiles and curls her finger in his wet hair. "You can do it now," she says. "Now we're courting."

"But am I, you know…"

"What?"

"Am I good enough?" he asks, the words blustering, his cheeks blushing.

Emma takes his hand and presses it against her breast. She curls her fingers around his neck and pulls him close. "Yes," she breathes into his ear.

Suddenly they hear voices drifting over the dunes and along the straw-strewn path to the beach. Emma scurries to pull her t-shirt on. Jacob brushes the sand from the blanket and packs his backpack, but then he stops.

"Should we go?"

Emma shrugs. "Maybe."

He nods, slings the pack on his back, and picks

up the helmets. He points towards the back of the bunker, and they run to the end and leap off into the dunes. Emma follows Jacob as they run towards the path, but then she stops as she sees the couple walking towards her. The woman sneers and points at Emma.

"That's the bitch from the car," she says.

Emma's stomach twists, and she takes a step back.

"Your dad could have killed us all. Where is he?"

"Emma?" Jacob looks at her. "What's going on?"

"You're Bo Falk's son," the man says.

"Yes."

The man jabs a finger at Emma. "What are you doing with that city bitch?"

"Hey," Jacob says. He juts out his chin as Emma retreats down the path towards the beach. "Watch what you're saying."

"Does your dad know you're here, with her?" the woman asks. "What would he say? What would he think?"

"She doesn't belong here," the man says. He raises his voice. "She belongs in the city. Go back to Copenhagen, bitch."

The man is older than Jacob's father, fatter, slower. Jacob drops the helmets and punches the man in the face. The woman swears and slaps at him. He shoves her out of the way and punches the man again. There is blood on the man's lip, it speckles Jacob's fist in gritty blobs of sand and blood.

"Come on," Jacob says, grabbing Emma's hand, pulling her past the woman, who is now cradling the man's head in her hands.

"Jacob," Emma shouts, as they reach the moped.

"The helmets, you dropped them back there."

He shakes his head, "we can't go back now." He fumbles the key from the pocket of his backpack, and starts the motor. Emma climbs onto the seat behind him, wraps her arms around his waist and presses her chin to his shoulder. Jacob walks the moped off its stand, turns, and accelerates up the gravel path, past a silver car with the bumper duct-taped to the side panel, and turns onto the cycle path. Emma shivers behind him. She wipes tears from her cheeks on his shirt as he drives home.

He stops in a lay-by before the entrance to the farm and turns off the motor.

"We need to walk," he says. "If mum sees us without helmets…"

"Okay." Emma climbs off the seat and stands beside the moped.

"Who were they, Emma?"

She shrugs. "I don't know."

"But they know you and your dad."

"They tried to shoot a wolf last night. Dad stopped them."

Jacob whistles when she tells him what happened.

"It's the wolves," she says. "Look what they make you do."

"We should go and check the wolves," he says. "Make sure they are all right."

Jacob leads the way to the Holloway, lifting the brambles with a stick as Emma crawls through the entrance. She waits for him, sweat running through the salt on her face, as Jacob smiles and brushes past her. The tunnel seems thinner in the daylight, as the sun streams through the brambles, lighting the tips of the thorns with splinters of white. Emma stops Jacob with a hand on his ankle. She shakes and he pulls her close, the thorns twisting in his hair as she sniffles into his shoulder.

"Sorry," she says, as she wipes at the snot on his shirt.

"It's alright."

"I was scared. I didn't know what they would do."

"Well, I kind of did it for them, if you know what I mean."

"You hit him, Jacob."

"He shouldn't have said what he did."

"Kind of heroic," she says, and smiles.

Jacob brushes her hair from her cheek. "Ready?"

She nods, and they crawl along the Holloway. The end of the tunnel is like a hide or a duck blind, the perfect place to observe without being seen. The bunker seems further away than the first time she saw it. The thick concrete walls are harder to see, less defined. Where the moonlight cast the bunker in sharp-edged shadow, the sun shines on the twist of old vines, yellowed leaves, and thick grasses. The grass is flat outside the den where the wolves tumble and sleep, but there is no sign of activity. The den is empty.

"Have they gone?" Emma whispers.

"I don't know."

"Should we go?"

"Probably, yes, it's almost lunchtime."

Jacob leads Emma across the field, away from the Holloway, holding her hand and brushing sand and soil from her arm. The sun bakes the last of the sea from their hair, and he points at the first sight of the farmhouse in a gap between the trees. He drops his arm to his side when he sees Bo up ahead.

"Is that your dad?" Emma asks, sensing Jacob tensing.

"Yes."

Bo waits for them. He takes Jacob by the arm and pulls him away from Emma. She can't hear what he says, but the crease in his lip, and the way he grips Jacob's arm chills her. She wants to look but turns away as he catches her eye. Bo lets go, pushing Jacob's shoulder, as they walk towards the farmhouse. Emma follows.

She sees the silver car with the battered bumper first and stops. Men are shouting in the courtyard. She hears her father's voice, recognises the man from the beach, and then sees the police car parked beside her father's Toyota. Bo leads Jacob across the courtyard, and the man raises his voice.

"He hit me, Bo. Smacked me in the face."

"And why did he do that, eh?"

"Because he's as stupid as his father," the woman says. Her voice echoes between the farm buildings. "You might think you're somebody, Bo Falk. But you're nothing, can't even run a farm properly." She spits as Bo takes a step towards her.

"Bo, don't," Camilla says, as she reaches for Jacob's hand and pulls him to her side.

The policemen work their way between the woman and Bo, hands on their belts, appealing for cool heads, despite the heat. Emma looks for her father and sees him standing next to Camilla. He says something when he sees her, but she doesn't stop to listen and then she runs, slipping on the cobblestones, kicking off her sandals and running barefoot across the paddock, scattering the sheep. She stops at the electric fence, catches a jolt in her shoulder and gasps as she crawls between the two metal wires, climbs the stile and runs across the field. She ignores her father's shouts and flees between the corn stubble. The church is in the distance, shining white on a hilltop, and Emma runs towards it.

She stops at the gate, wipes at the tears on her cheeks, and limps up the path across the gravel to the church door. The door is in shadow, the handle heavy and cool in her grasp. Emma closes it behind her, her feet slapping on the cool stone floor as she walks to the altar and slides onto a pew. Emma clenches her fists and presses her knuckles into her legs.

Emma doesn't hear the priest walking between the pews. She doesn't hear the creak of the wood as he sits down beside her. She twitches her nose at the smell of tobacco clinging to his robes but says nothing. Her skin is white beneath her knuckles. Emma stares at the white wall behind the altar, and the cross hanging above it.

"I can't remember the last time I saw someone in my church on a Friday lunchtime," Aage says.

Emma's fingers shake as she stretches them. She makes fists, then smoothes her hands flat against her legs, rolling sand and salt beneath her palms.

"I've never done it," she says.

"What's that, child?"

"Sex. Jacob thinks I've had sex. I haven't."

"That's okay."

"No, it's not," she says. "He might not want to. He might think…"

Aage is quiet, like the church. Emma rubs her hands back and forth. The sand scratches her skin.

"Emma," Aage says. "Why have you come?"

She lifts her chin, wipes a tear from her cheek, and bunches her fists.

"It's not about him, is it, Emma?"

She shakes her head.

"But he is important to you. You care about him."

"Yes," she says. "And today I got him into trouble."

"You did?"

"Yes. Because of what happened last night. Because of the wolf."

"That was unfortunate," Aage says.

"You know about it?"

"Of course, that's why I came to your house, by the beach. I was waiting. I wanted to talk to your father. I left him a note, but he hasn't called." Aage takes a long breath. "And now you are here."

Emma sniffs. She wraps her arms across her chest.

"It's cold," she says.

"It is cool in here." Aage points towards the room to one side of the altar. "I have a fleece in there. Wait here, I'll go and get it."

The pew creaks as Aage stands up. Emma presses her hand into the pocket of her shorts.

"Shit."

Aage frowns as he returns with a fleece jacket. He drapes it over the pew in front of Emma.

"Sorry," she says. "I left my phone in Jacob's backpack."

"I'm sure he'll find it."

Emma nods and pulls on the jacket. "Thank you," she says.

"Shall we talk? I might be able to help you, and

you can help me, I'm sure of it." He sits down. "You'll find I'm very easy to talk to, about all kinds of things. I have help, you see," he says, with a nod towards the cross. "Of course, sometimes I need help too. He helps me help others, especially when things are muddled, and cloudy, as they are now. Especially now."

"Things are all muddled," Emma says.

"That's right. And when they are like that – all muddled – it takes strength to find the cause of it all, Emma, to know when to do the right thing. I think you know what I'm talking about, don't you?" He smiles at Emma and places a gentle hand on her shoulder. "Just think, Emma, all these problems would be gone, if we just got rid of a few bad eggs. I think you might know where those eggs are. And, if you want to do the right thing, if you want to help your father, make things right with Jacob, perhaps you can tell me?"

Chapter 18

Jon parks his car beside Aage's and jogs down to the beach. He sees the priest at the water's edge and shields his eyes from the sun.

"She's not here, Jon," Aage says.

"I don't understand. You said she was with you."

"She is with me." Aage points along the beach towards Thyrup. "I thought it would be best if we spoke alone."

"About Emma?"

"About many things."

"No," Jon says. "That's not good enough. You might think you have some weight in the community, but I'm not from Thyrup, neither is Emma. So, you tell me where she is, right now."

"I told you she is with me. She's at the church, gardening, if you can believe it." Aage smiles. "We walked around the cemetery, had a long talk. It was good for her. She needed to get a lot of things off her chest. We stopped by one of the graves and I told her about the woman that was buried there. A young woman, not much older than Emma, who died hundreds of years ago. They were difficult times. Some say that she was driven mad, that the people from the village drove her mad. When I told Emma this, she started to pluck at the weeds. That's where I left her. She's fine, Jon. A little upset, but fine. It's you I'm worried about."

"Jacob has her phone. It's the first time she's never had it on her. I can't call her."

"Did you hear what I said?"

"I need to see her."

"Walk with me first. Emma is fine. *You* need to

talk."

Aage stops to look at a starfish. He picks it up and throws it back into the sea.

"You've heard the story?" he asks. "About the boy on a beach full of starfish. There are so many, drowning on the sand. He's throwing them, one by one, into the water. But there are so many, and a couple on the beach stop him and say it's hopeless. He can't possibly save them all." Aage stops and places his hand on Jon's arm. "The boy throws another starfish into the sea. Do you know what he says?"

"It matters to that one," Jon says. "I've heard it before."

"Loren Eiseley," Aage says. "He was American, you know?"

"Why are you telling me this?"

"The wolves."

"Yes?"

"It matters."

"I know it does. That's why I rammed that car in the field."

"You rammed a car, Emma is distraught, and Jacob is in trouble with the police."

"But it matters to that wolf."

"You didn't listen to the story. The wolves are not the starfish, Jon, we are." Aage skips to one side as the surf surges onto the beach. "Thyrup is drowning. Which is ironic, when you think we haven't had a drop of rain in fifty days. We've talked about this before, but now, with you hitting the car, and Olivia and her friend threatening Camilla like that…"

"They were looking for Bo."

"And threatening Camilla, she told me. Then

there's Anton, my own son, nearly killed by a wolf – because of it attacking him. This can't go on. Don't you see?"

Jon stops as the surf curls in front of his feet. If they kept walking they would arrive at the beach house. He looks over his shoulder, back towards his car. *Emma is at the church*, he thinks. Aage cups his hands around a cigarette and lights it. The smoke drifts past Jon's nose.

"There's no smoke without fire," Jon says.

"Exactly."

"You want me to change my opinion of the bite marks."

"Viktoria is very busy, Jon, but with a wildlife biologist in the village – well she needs your support, your experience. She's very young."

"But what will it matter?"

Aage laughs. "It sounds like a cliché, but *it will matter to her*," he says. "It will matter to us all. If you agree with her findings, then, together with what happened to Anton, the ministry will have no choice but to conclude that the wolves are problem wolves, and they can act accordingly."

"We don't even know how many there are."

"Five, according to Emma."

"What?"

"She has seen them. She won't say where, of course, but she has seen two adults and a litter of three cubs."

"She never said anything."

"Ah, that's love for you. Jacob swore her to secrecy. Another little irony, don't you think? I mean, just think if Bo knew his own son knew the location of the wolf den… I can't imagine what he would do."

"She thinks you will keep it secret, because you are a priest."

"I am Lutheran, Jon, it wasn't a confession. I have a duty to my flock, to keep them safe from harm."

"You're a bastard. She trusted you."

"And now, you have to trust me, don't you?"

The surf surges up the beach and soaks Jon's shoes. He considers pushing the priest into the water, but he knows it won't change anything. As the water sinks and bubbles into the sand, Jon stares at Aage finishing his cigarette, extinguishing it with a pinch of his fingers.

"What do you want me to do?"

"Tell the truth, Jon. Pass on your recommendations to Christiansborg; urge them to take action before the end of the summer. Act now while the media is on our side, before something tragic happens."

"Like what happened to Anton?"

Aage turns and walks back towards their cars, slowly until Jon catches up with him.

"I have arranged for Lærke to talk to you," Aage says. "She was disappointed that you interrupted her interview with Emma, but…" he says, and points to the satellite dish mounted to the roof of the DR van, just visible between the dunes. "There she is now. Just in time to broadcast live for the evening news, I think."

"You've got it all planned, haven't you?"

"Bo might have shown some muscle at the town meeting, but it's important that you understand *who* is really in control here in Thyrup, Jon. I can be very helpful, but you don't want me as an enemy. And, if my flock is threatened, if you are part of the threat, then you will find I am a very powerful enemy, not easily defeated."

The camera crew follow Lærke through the dunes and onto the beach. Jon sees that the satellite dish is raised, assorted antennae extended.

"Lærke doesn't know about your adventures last night, Jon. Not yet. So, why don't you start by telling her that you have revisited your findings, and can now confirm that you agree with Viktoria, that the bite marks are those of the wolf? That would be a good start."

Jon starts to walk and Aage stops him.

"After the interview, I think it is very important that you talk with your daughter. Because, when the wolves are declared a problem, and when the hunter is called in to shoot them, he needs to know where to find the den. Emma knows. If she doesn't tell you, then I will have to tell Bo that his son is keeping a dreadful secret. Bo is a very driven man, very committed. He will take it hard. I don't like to think what will happen to Jacob. But, still, that will be nothing compared to Emma's pain. The young just don't have the experience to bear the pain that adults do. To be young and to betray a young love." Aage sighs, as Lærke walks towards them. "A tragedy. She will be crushed, and she will hate herself, perhaps almost as much as she will hate you."

"Me?"

"You did bring her here, Jon."

Aage lingers out of shot as Lærke interviews Jon. It is live. He knows his phone will ring the second he is off air. Jon glares at Aage as the camera operator moves to focus on Lærke as she answers the news anchor's questions from the studio. He half hears the debate, ignores the heat flushing his skin as his own words are debated back and forth in this *surprising new development from Thyrup*. He slips away, out of camera shot, striding towards the parking area. Aage says something, but Jon ignores him. He gets in his car and drives to the end of the beach road and stops. His phone rings. He recognises Felix's number and swipes the screen to end the call.

Then Jon calls Camilla and she answers on the second ring.

"Is Emma with you?"

"Yes," she says. "She and Jacob are in the paddock. I can go and get her."

"No. It's okay. I'll come and pick her up. Just tell her to stay there."

Jon digs his hand in his pocket and pulls out David McGrath's business card. He dials the number and listens, the dial tone reminds him of a soft warble, lasting just a second longer than it should before clicking and recycling.

"David?" he says, when the dial tone stops. "It's Jon, from Denmark. Is this a good time?"

"It's early," David says. "But it's okay. Let me pour my coffee."

Jon winds the window down and turns his head to one side as the television van and Aage drive past. He ignores the priest's wave.

"Right, I'm on the deck, got my coffee," David says. "What do you need?"

"Help, as much as you can give me."

"People problems?"

"How did you guess?"

"You're dealing with wolves. You can't have one

without the other."

Jon waits as David slurps his coffee.

"Let me guess, they went all crazy and caught you off guard, didn't they?"

"Not just them," Jon says. "I kind of went crazy too."

"Sounds about right," David says. He chuckles for a second, takes another slurp of coffee. "I told you to look ahead, to anticipate where the wolves are going. The same works for people, too. Where are they going, Jon?"

"They're going for the den."

"You're sure about that?"

"They want the right to shoot the wolves, and they want me to help them do that."

"They'll shoot them anyway. If they find the den, they'll burn the cubs out, trap the entrance, and gut the adults. I've seen men tie ropes around the legs of a gut-shot wolf and drag it apart with snowmobiles. It doesn't stop at the killing, Jon, they need to *exorcise* themselves."

"You mean the wolf."

"No. I mean them. The wolf is just a means to an end. You need to understand that. How else do you explain irrational fear? Have you thrown the statistics at them yet? Deaths on the road against deaths by wolf, or bee, or lightning?"

"I didn't have to."

"That's because they've already got it all figured out. Everything they read makes sense. It's like terrorists interpreting the Bible or the Koran, or whatever Cool Aid they're drinking. If they don't like what they're reading, or what you're saying, they'll cut and paste it until it makes sense. They've probably rearranged everything you said already, just so it fits."

Jon shakes his head. He swallows past the lump in his throat, licks his dry lips.

"That's exactly what happened. I suppose I should go and move the wolves from the den."

"You've got about as much right to do that as they have to kill them. Where will you put them, Jon? In a zoo? Hell, you may as well shoot them yourself. Wild animals aren't built for zoos. You ever seen a lone wolf excluded from the pack?"

"Yes."

"They kick them out of their territory; kill them if they cross that line. Where do you think they send outcasts in a zoo? They push them closest to the door, closest to the humans. You can't remove the wolves, you can't fence them in or out, you sure as hell can't put them in a zoo."

"Then what *can* I do?"

The wind whistling across David's deck at his cabin outside Fairbanks cuts into the line with a blast of static. Jon catches a few words before the line is cut and the call ends. He knows what David said, even without hearing it. He knows what he has to do. He just wonders if it will matter in the end, or if the wolf even cares.

Chapter 19

Jon can't remember Emma ever hugging him so tightly and for so long. He strokes her back, kisses her on top of her head, and walks her to the car. Jacob watches from the window of the farmhouse.

"She can stay the night," Camilla says.

"Would you like that, Emma?"

"Maybe tomorrow," she says, as Jacob steps out of the farmhouse. "I'll call."

He nods and stuffs his hands in his pockets. He stands there until they are almost at the road. Jon sees him in the mirror.

"I thought we should try again, – to find that special restaurant," he says. "But maybe somewhere bigger this time."

"Bigger?"

"Than Thyrup. There's a Greek restaurant in Skive, if you fancy that. It's a bit of a drive."

"If it means we're away for longer then, yes, that would be good."

"I brought you some clothes from the beach house, or we can go back, and you can change."

"It's fine, I can change in the toilets or something."

"Okay."

There is smoke on the horizon and the traffic slows as they pass the last flames of a corn fire. The police direct them onto a smaller road, and Emma uses her GPS to get them to Skive. The music in the restaurant makes her smile, and Jon relaxes as they are shown to a table, and Emma sneaks to the bathroom. She has clean clothes on when she returns and kisses her father on the cheek.

"Thanks," she says.

"I thought you might want something different. You've been wearing those shorts and that t-shirt the past two days."

"It's so hot. You wear something and it just gets sticky."

They don't talk until the main course, and Jon wonders if she will tell him about the den. He decides it's his turn to confess what he talked about with the priest.

"Emma," he says. "I have a problem."

"The people in the car? The one you drove into?" Emma's face pales, her fork trembles in her hand.

"No, they never filed a complaint, or pressed charges, or whatever it is they could have done. They know we stopped them doing something illegal."

"But Jacob…"

"Yes, I know. He's being charged with assault. And I am so sorry, Emma. It's my fault."

"He doesn't blame you. He said so." She stops trembling and laughs. "He thinks we're crazy, and I think he feels part of it, now that he did something crazy too."

Jon orders more water and Emma asks for a coke as the waiter passes the table. They listen to the music for a moment, travelling back in time four years to another hot summer in Greece, another time when he made Emma's life difficult.

"It's alright, dad," she says. "I know why you left mum."

"How did you know I was thinking about that?"

"We're in a Greek restaurant in July. It wasn't a stretch."

"I suppose not."

Emma waits as the waiter brings their drinks. She remembers her parents fighting that night in the hotel room, muffled voices and the hiss of accusation rolled around the walls, whispering into Emma's room like an evil wind. She remembers being impressed at their restraint, how they could fight so quietly.

"I've got a problem, too, dad."

He rests his fork on his plate and waits.

"I told the priest something, and I wish I hadn't."

"That's okay."

"No, it's not. If I was going to tell anyone, it should have been you."

"Can you tell me now?"

"I want to," she says. "But I don't know what you will do."

Jon looks at his watch. "How about you wait and tell me until we've been somewhere else."

"Where?"

"The hospital, in Skive. I checked the visiting hours. I'd like to go and see Anton. Did you know that the priest is his father?"

"Yes."

"The priest is my problem, one of them, and I think Anton can help."

"Is that why we came to Skive?"

Jon presses his lips into a flat smile. "Yes," he says. "I'm sorry, but it *is* the closest Greek restaurant."

"It's okay," she says. "It's good to get away."

Anton is in the hospital cafeteria, he waves at them as they walk through the entrance. Jon squeezes Emma's shoulder, whispering a quick thank you before greeting Anton. Jon fields a few looks as some of the patients recognise his face, and the word *wolves* bounces between the tables.

"You're famous," Anton says.

"We both are. This is my daughter, Emma."

"I thought I recognised you." Anton winces as he shakes her hand. "Sorry, the ribs are still knitting together."

"Anton," Jon says, "I have a problem."

"I saw the news. You've changed your mind?"

"I had help."

"Let me guess, my father got to you?"

"Yes."

"He's a manipulative sod. It was him who convinced me to say it was a wolf that attacked me."

"You don't think it was?"

"It was a bloody great Alsatian. Wild and more frightening than the wolves. I thought it probably had rabies, which is stupid, because we don't have rabies in Denmark."

"Only in bats."

"Well, they have me on a course of rabies shots anyway." Anton pushes back a chair and lifts his leg onto it. He bites his lip as he peels back a square plaster the length and width of his hand. "My dad told me not to show it to you. But, it's the least I can do." Anton lets the plaster fold onto his ankle as Jon stands up to have a closer look.

"Can I?" he says and takes out his phone.

"Sure."

Jon takes the teaspoon from Anton's saucer and holds it next to the bite. He takes a picture. The wound is clean, and the skin is starting to pinch together. Anton encouraged blood to flow when he removed the bandage and now it pools in the holes in the skin.

"They're not deep enough for a wolf," Jon says, as he points. "This area here should be more bruised with deeper haemorrhaging if the jaws had clamped down. It looks like whatever bit you…"

"A big dog."

Jon nods. "It had bad teeth. Cracked or chipped. It's not unusual for wolves to break their incisors, but then there would have been more crushing. A deer can't run on a broken leg."

Emma excuses herself to buy something from the cafeteria as the woman serving announces they are closing in ten minutes. Jon watches her pull out her phone.

"She's fallen for the boy next door."

"What's that?" Anton says, as he covers his wound with the bandage.

"Emma is seeing your neighbour's son."

"Jacob Falk? He's a good kid. A bit shy."

"His mum said the same, although I think Emma's bringing him out of his shell."

Emma browses the cakes, waves to catch Jon's eye, and then gestures with her mobile that she is going outside. Jon's chair squeaks across the tiled floor as he sits down.

"So, we agree," Anton says. "I was bitten by a dog."

"And trampled by a herd of cattle. You're lucky to be alive."

"Aage wants me to give an interview. He tried sending the journalist, Tilde Sørensen, to the hospital, but I told the nurses to keep her away. This is the first time I have been off the ward. My wife, Maja, is coming tomorrow to take me home."

"That's good."

"I think my ribs will hurt just as much wherever I am. I may as well be at home. There's so much to do, although, I can't exactly *do* anything. Maja has been working twelve-hour days since the accident, not including the drive up and down to visit me."

"This dog," Jon says. "Could it be local?"

"There are plenty of dogs in the area, but I didn't recognise this one. It could have been one of the tourists' dogs. It happens every summer – a dog runs away from the summer houses by the beach, scares some sheep, maybe even bites one or two, before they catch it again. But, this wasn't the kind of dog anyone would have as a pet."

"I think it's Bo's dog."

"He doesn't have a dog."

"I saw him buy dog food in a village outside Thyrup, and I found a chain and pellets in a shed at the back of his house. I think it's his."

"When?"

"I saw the shed earlier today."

"But how long has he had it?"

"When I asked him he denied it. He says he doesn't have one. But what if the dog got free," Jon says. He lowers his voice as Emma walks through the automatic doors.

"You think Bo's dog attacked me?"

"I think if a dog attacked you – and we both think it was a dog – then it's better to have people think it was a wolf. It's very convenient too. For some people."

"Like my father," Anton says. "Jesus."

Jon waves at Emma. "Just give me a second," he says. He lowers his voice. "Would you recognise the dog if I found it?"

"Yes."

"And would you say as much, publicly? Even if it means going against your father?"

"There's not much love there. He caught me when I was weak, right after the accident," Anton says and shrugs, then makes a face as he remembers his ribs. "Sure. Whatever you need. But what are you trying to do?"

"Aage has been quick to cry wolf at every opportunity. He is feeding the media with news and developments. He seems to have Tilde Sørensen in his pocket."

"That doesn't surprise me. Tilde used to be a regular at the church, back when I used to go. You have a theory?"

"More of a plan. If I can call Aage out, publicly, prove that the wolf attacks were dogs, then maybe there's a chance."

"To do what? Save the wolf? Jon, you still haven't got it, have you? Thyrup doesn't need an actual wolf to see *wolves*. I mean, sure, there *are* wolves in Thyrup, but hardly anyone has seen one. The idea of the wolf is enough, and that's what my father preys on – ideas and fear. He's an old man struggling to keep up with a modern world. His congregation is dwindling, and he lives in fear of the church replacing him with a younger and, God forbid, female priest." Anton laughed. "His worst nightmare. The biggest wolf in Thyrup is my father – he's the leader of the pack, or the *flock* as he calls them. He's terrified that he'll lose the top slot."

"To save the wolf I'm going to have to give them another. You understand what that means?"

"Hey," Anton says, and points at his leg. "My

father told me to lie to help his cause. I can't help thinking that he might have liked it even more if I had died. As it is he's got video of a helicopter, a Hollywood rescue, and police crawling all over the farm. If he knew about a dog, even if he is just covering up for Bo, then he deserves what he gets. Just tell me what to say, when to say it, and I'll be there."

"Thanks. It means a lot."

"Hey, the first time I met you was in the middle of my field with a beater. I don't remember seeing him there, do you?"

Jon shakes Anton's hand as he stands up. The cafeteria staff roll down the metal blinds, and Anton shuffles back to the elevator. It's dark outside, but the glow of Emma's mobile lights up her face, and Jon sees a sparkle in her eyes. *It's probably Jacob*, he thinks, and wonders just how he might dissuade her from spending the night at Falk farm.

"Is that Jacob?" he says, as he unlocks the car.

"Pernille," she says. "From my class?"

"I know Pernille. Is she back in Denmark?"

"They got home yesterday. We were just catching up. She's got an amazing tan."

Jon fastens his seatbelt as Emma gets into the car.

"Do you think she'd like a few days on the beach? I can pay for her ticket."

"That's sweet, dad, but I think she just wants to see her boyfriend."

"Okay, but if she wanted to, or any of your other friends…"

"I know what you're doing, dad."

"What's that?"

"You're trying to stop me seeing so much of

Jacob."

"You have seen a lot of him these past few days."

Emma says nothing, and Jon starts the car. He pats her knee and mouths the word *sorry* before turning onto the main road.

"You were going to tell me something earlier," he says.

"It can wait."

"You're sure?"

"Yes, let's go home – to the beach house."

"You don't want to stay the night at Jacob's?"

"Not tonight. He sent me a text. He's busy helping his dad with something."

Chapter 20

Jacob holds the torch as Bo loads the rifle. The wind is still and the sweat trickles down Jacob's neck. His father said they had to wait until dark. He didn't say for what, but Jacob knows. He saw the shed door, open, swinging on its hinges. The dog is loose, again. Bo chambers a round in the rifle, flicks the safety catch on, and nods for Jacob to start walking.

"Maja told your mum she saw a wolf in the fields when she was finished with the herd."

"And that's what we're looking for?"

"Don't be stupid, Jacob. You know we're looking for that bloody dog." Bo slings the rifle over his shoulder and takes the torch from Jacob's hand. There is a rustling in the bushes and he prods Jacob forwards. Jacob uncoils the rope from his hand and then freezes as a raccoon dog races out of the bushes. There are two of them and they scatter across the field. He grins at his father and Bo gestures for him to keep walking.

It occurs to Jacob, as he walks twenty metres ahead of his father, that he is the bait. He doesn't doubt his father would shoot a wolf, if he had the chance. He wonders if he would shoot the dog. *Of the two, it's the dog that is more dangerous*, he thinks.

Something snaps in the undergrowth, heavy feet, and big paws, enough to make Jacob stop. His skin cools and he runs his hand across the hairs on his arm. It's the first time all day that he has felt comfortable in the heat, but it doesn't last, because when he sees the eyes shining in the undergrowth, he runs.

"Jacob," Bo shouts.

Jacob wonders if his father will shoot if he is in front of the dog, or even the wolf. But it is a fleeting thought. The beast is close; he can hear the scratch of its claws as it races across the earth. The moon hides behind a cloud and the field darkens. Jacob leaps into the hedgerow on the other side of the field. The light from the torch bobs in his father's hand, but then Jacob feels the first snap of teeth as the beast bites at the air immediately behind his back. Jacob crashes through the hedge, rips his skin on a hawthorn, scrabbles up and onto the field on the other side. He can see the church and runs towards it.

There's another light bobbing up the hill on the track towards the church. Jacob turns and runs towards it. He risks a glance over his shoulder, sees the dog – *their* dog – tugging at the thin branches of the hawthorn tree tangled in its fur. It breaks free as Jacob reaches the end of the field.

There's a gap in the trees and Jacob crashes through it, stumbling onto the path to the church. The light is still there; it's someone out for a walk. Jacob runs towards the light, wills his legs to pump faster as he hears the dog skitter onto the gravel path. It chases him up the path, and the light ahead of them lifts. The man shines his torch into Jacob's eyes, and then the dog's.

"Run," Jacob shouts.

He doesn't recognise him as he bumps past. There is a shout, a scuffle of gravel and dirt and then a thump. Jacob turns, as the man's torch tumbles to the path, the light extinguished as the batteries slip out of the handle. Jacob takes a step towards the man, but freezes at the sight of the dog, its teeth clamped around the man's throat as it squeezes and tugs the man's neck from one side to the other.

"Jacob," Bo shouts, and throws him the rope.

The rope slaps against Jacob's chest and he grabs it, as his dad slips the rifle off his shoulder and slams it into the dog's head, again and again, until it slumps on the man's body and Bo drags it by the hind legs onto the path.

"Put the rope around its neck," Bo says.

Jacob lifts the dog's head with the toe of his boot. Its bloody tongue lolls to one side. The eyes are misty. Jacob looks at its chest, sees the ribs rising and falling beneath the thick mat of fur and blood, and he ties a knot around its neck. It's the same knot he uses to lash things to the trailer. He knows it is tight, that the dog can't bite it, but he loops it once more around the dog's front and back paws on one side, cinching them together with another knot in the middle of the rope. When the dog is secure he turns to help his dad.

Bo stands next to the man who is spluttering at his feet. The man's eyes are wide. He is dying.

"Dad?"

"Shut up, Jacob." Bo takes Jacob's arm, and pulls him to one side, pointing at the church. "Take the dog to the back of the church. There's a garage for tools; the door is unlocked. Put it in there, keep it tied up."

"What about that man?"

"Come back when you've done it."

"He's dying, dad."

Bo slaps Jacob's cheek. He points at the dog and turns his back on him. Jacob slides his arms under the dog and carries it up the path. He feels the dog's quick breaths, can smell the man's blood around its jaw. The church gate swings open and Jacob's boots crunch along the path to the back of the church. He puts the dog inside the tool shed, looks at its eyes and turns away. He can't look at it. It's eyes are pleading and Jacob is too frightened to help. *Just like dad*, he thinks, as he shuts the door.

Bo meets him at the gate, presses his hand against Jacob's chest and tells him to wait.

"What for?"

"Just wait," Bo says, and glances down the path. "It'll be over soon."

They both hear the sigh, a last slough of breath leaking out of the dead man. Bo nods for Jacob to follow him, and they walk down the path. The man's eyes are still open, but it's easier to look at him now that he is dead.

"Who is he, dad?"

"I don't know. He could be a tourist."

"Shouldn't we…"

Bo curls his arm around Jacob's neck and walks him down the path. Jacob feels the stubble on his father's chin pressing into his cheek.

"It was a wolf. That's what they'll say when they find him. Do you understand?"

"Yes," Jacob breathes.

"Say you understand."

"I understand, dad, I do. It was a wolf."

"Good boy." Bo lets go and Jacob staggers to the opposite side of the path. "Go home Jacob. Clean up. Have a shower. Get mum to wash your clothes." Bo presses the rifle into Jacob's hands.

"Where are you going?"

"To muzzle the dog. You didn't do that, did you?"

Jacob shakes his head.

"When the police come, if they hear the dog whining, it'll all be over."

"Why don't we just kill the dog, dad? Bury it."

"No. Not yet."

Jacob leaves his father on the path. *He's gone mad*, he thinks. He wouldn't have done that a year ago. It's the heat. The drought. Jacob stumbles into the field. It's the wolves. The rifle is heavy in his hands. He turns away from the house and runs across the first field, and the next, until he finds the bramble entrance to the Holloway. He knows what he has to do. Jacob pushes the rifle through the brambles and crawls into the tunnel. His heart hurts inside his chest, as if it will beat through his ribs. But he understands now, he knows the root of the evil that has infected his father, the priest, the village. Jacob lifts the rifle and flicks the safety off with a soft click. There is a flicker of movement and he sees the female, the mother, as she rests outside the den. They are back, and if he kills the two adults, then he can find the cubs. He thinks about keeping them, hiding them in the barn, but he knows his father will find them. *Better to kill them now*, he thinks. *All of them*.

It's hot inside the bramble tunnel. Jacob wipes at the sweat on his brow, feels the sting of salt in his eyes. He moves the rifle, focuses the iron sight at the end of the barrel on the female's chest. But he can't see. His eyes sting, but it's not sweat, he knows he is crying. The rifle presses against the bramble branches, twitching up and down as he sobs, breathes, sucks air past the spittle on his lips. Snot streams from his nose and he wipes it away. The female sniffs again, and Jacob sinks to the floor of the tunnel, dragging the rifle with him, until he is curled, the barrel of the rifle just inches from his own skull. He thinks about pulling the trigger.

Jacob bites back a scream as he replays the image of the dog mauling the man, the dog's eyes, the sound of the man sighing his last breath. He lowers the rifle, leans his head against the barrel, sees another face – the man he punched on the path. It's all too much. The images play on repeat, and he sinks to the warm earth floor of the Holloway and squeezes his eyes shut.

Jacob sleeps until the hour before dawn. When he wakes the wolves are gone. Perhaps they have gone, for good. Jacob doesn't think so, the cubs are still so small, too small to travel long distances. He crawls out of the tunnel and into the field. He slings the rifle over his shoulder and walks home.

The lights are on in the farmhouse, and Jacob sees his father sitting at the kitchen table. His mother is at the sink. When Camilla sees Jacob, she opens the door and wraps her arms around him. She holds him for five minutes before Bo steps out of the kitchen, prises her hands away from Jacob and takes the rifle from his shoulder.

"Jacob," he says. "Something terrible has happened. A man has been killed by a wolf, over by the church. Your mother has been worried sick. I told her you were with Emma."

"But why are you covered in dirt," Camilla says. "Why are you carrying a gun?"

"He just wanted to impress her," Bo says. "That's right isn't it?"

Jacob nods.

"Good boy. Now go inside. Get cleaned up. We'll have breakfast."

Jacob turns on the shower and steps into the cubicle. The water tugs at his shirt, fills the pockets of his jeans, sluices the dirt, blood and fur from his boots. He doesn't hear his mum call, not the first or the second time. She knocks on the bathroom door, holds her breath for a second, and then reaches past him to turn off the water.

He can't remember the last time his mother removed his clothes or towelled him dry. He doesn't care. All he can see is a path with a dead man, blood at his throat. He sees a dog, bound and muzzled, gagged, behind a lawnmower in the church tool shed. He sees wolves napping, playing, tumbling, and licking outside a bunker, and he sees Emma, naked, covered in blood, and he screams.

"Shh, Jacob," Camilla says. She curls him into her body, kicks the door closed as Bo charges down the hall. She lowers Jacob to the floor, cradles his head, strokes his hair, rocks him until the screams subside, and he rests his head on her shoulder.

Later, at the hospital, the doctors say he might be dehydrated.

"Dehydrated?" Camilla almost laughs; it's shock. She has never seen her boy like this.

"Is he drinking enough?"

They say it was typical among young people.

"They either drink too much or too little," they say.

Jacob doesn't hear them, doesn't see them. It's only when the doctors leave and his mother says he has a visitor, only when Emma takes his hand, when she strokes his fingers, kisses him lightly on the cheek, only then does he look up.

"It was a wolf," he says.

Chapter 21

Jon looks at his daughter framed within the tiny window of the door to Jacob's room. Jon yawns, tips the last dregs of coffee into his mouth and walks along the corridor towards the hospital cafeteria. The staff are busy preparing breakfast behind the metal blinds, and he finds Camilla at the drinks machine. She fumbles coins from her purse, swearing as they clatter to the floor and spin beneath the machine, out of sight.

"Let me," Jon says, and presses a ten kroner coin into the slot. "Coffee?"

"Tea," she says, and wipes the cuff of her thin blouse across her eyes.

Jon carries the drinks to a table. He can smell the bread rolls in the oven, and his stomach grumbles.

"It's good of you to come," Camilla says.

"Of course."

"Emma means so much to him."

"Yes."

Camilla turns the cup in her hands, runs her nails up and down the thin plastic ribs. "He was out all night, Jon. I don't understand. He had Bo's gun. I think he was going to kill himself. My son. Why would he do that?"

"I don't know. But, he didn't, Camilla. And you've done the right thing, bringing him here."

"They think he is dehydrated. Can you believe it?"

There is a flutter of movement behind the blinds, and then the shudder of metal as the blinds are rolled up and the cafeteria opens. The smell of bread rolls is stronger now, and Jon rises only to stop at the buzz of his mobile.

"It's the police," he says, as he reads the text. "There's been another attack. They want me to look at the bite mark."

"Bo said the police found a man this morning, a jogger found him on the church path," Camilla says.

"I have to go." Jon glances towards the ward.

"I can bring Emma back, if you don't mind her staying. I think it will be good for Jacob."

"I don't mind. She can call me later, when she wants to be picked up. How will you get back?"

"I have the car. Bo is at the farm. He has a field to cut."

Jon nods. He buys another coffee and two buttered rolls on his way out, crumbling and flaking the crust into his lap as he drives south and west to Thyrup. He squints each time the sun flashes in the mirror, turns on the air conditioning and the radio. The airwaves are electric with the reports of a man's death in wolf country. The presenters remember the attack on Anton, how he was almost killed, but that was cattle, they say, this was a wolf. This is the death they have all been waiting for, the death Aage needs to bring his flock deeper into the fold. Jon considers calling Anton, remembers he has only been home one night, and decides to wait, at least until he has had a chance to examine the body.

He stops a few kilometres east of Thyrup, calls the police, and asks for directions. He frowns when they tell him the body is at the veterinary surgery. Jon arrives just a few minutes later, sees the television van and parks beside it. All the other spaces are occupied.

"Not now," he says, as Lærke asks him to comment. "Maybe after."

The police let him into the surgery and Jon finds Viktoria in the operating room. The man's body barely fits on the table.

"I've told them what I think," Viktoria says. "You'll say different, I'm sure."

"I haven't seen him yet."

Viktoria points at the dead man. "Be quick," she says. "I have patients this morning. Small animal surgery," she says, when Jon looks at her.

The man was strangled, his throat lacerated, and the air restricted. Jon peers closely at the holes in his neck. He turns his head as a detective joins him at the table.

"He choked on his own blood," the man says. "But we'll need an autopsy before we know for sure. I just wanted your opinion."

"You want to know if it was a wolf?"

"The vet says so."

Jon walks around the table to study the wound from another angle. "He was attacked on the path?"

"That's where he was found. His torch was in pieces. It makes sense that's where he was attacked."

"It makes no sense," Jon says, "for a wolf to attack a man on a church path. They are not opportunists. They hunt for their food. If they were crossing the path, they would run away if startled." Jon takes out his phone.

"What are you doing?"

"I took a photo of Anton's leg. I want to see if they are the same teeth."

Jon holds his mobile to one side of the dead man's neck. Viktoria looks over his shoulder.

"The left incisor is blunt," Jon says. He points at the screen, enlarges the photo, and turns it towards the detective and Viktoria. "The hole on the left side of the neck is deeper, the other one more ragged, just like Anton's leg."

"The same wolf," the detective says.

"The same animal." Jon slips his mobile into his pocket. "You keep saying wolf."

"What else can it be?"

"A dog can do that," Jon says.

"That's your opinion?"

"Yes."

Viktoria shakes her head as she leaves the room.

"Viktoria says it's a wolf. You say it's a dog," the detective says.

"I said a dog can do that. I'm not convinced it is a wolf."

The detective calls the policeman into the room and arranges for the body to be transported to the hospital mortuary. Then he asks for the photo of Anton's leg and Jon sends it to him. As soon as the detective has finished with him he makes his way back into the surgery to find Viktoria.

"You think I'm deliberately disagreeing with you, don't you?" he says.

"It doesn't matter," she says. "I'm not a doctor. I don't pronounce cause of death."

"But you think it was a wolf?"

"This isn't Greenland, Jon. The wolf doesn't have hundreds of empty kilometres to roam in. It's in the middle of a farming community, in the tourist belt. There's rumours of a den. What if there's a family of them now, a pack. Imagine that, a pack of wolves roaming in the woods where children play, where old people walk their dogs, tourists ride their bikes. Now a man has been killed by an animal on a church path.

Can't you see it? Can't you make the connection? If you agree with me and if the autopsy shows that the man – a tourist – died from the attack, then we can stop this. The government will be forced to act, the wolves will be killed, and Thyrup can try to save the rest of the tourist season before people start to leave." Viktoria points in the direction of the beach. "If this was a shark it would have been killed already."

"But it's not a shark, Viktoria. I'm not even sure it's a wolf."

"That's right, you think there's a wild dog out there, just roaming around attacking people."

"I didn't say it was roaming."

"No? You think it's hunting, is that it? Well, why don't you go out and find it. Find your wild dog, protect your bloody wolves, and leave us all alone. I think we all know that's for the best. You can at least agree with me about that, eh?"

Jon says nothing. He leaves the surgery, holding his hand up for no comment as he walks past the journalists. He gets in his car and drives away. He slows along the main street of Thyrup as tourists wait in a line at the bakery. He passes the house that Olivia and Sebastian have rented for the summer, sees Sebastian slide a long thin case into the back of a Land Rover. Sebastian stares at him as he drives past. The image lingers in Jon's mind until he slows at the turning for the church road. He drives slowly, stopping as a television van for a local channel backs out of the tiny church parking area. Jon takes the empty spot and gets out of the car.

He finds the bloody spot on the path, several metres from the gate to the church grounds. Yellow police tape marks the area, but Jon can see around it and below it. There is a lot of blood.

Blood trails were easy to follow in Greenland, although the Arctic wolves preyed on smaller animals. Jon used to joke with his guide, priding himself on finding a trail, until the snow covered it and he relied on Inuk to show him where new snow filled wolf prints, and guiding him to where he anticipated the wolf to be, the likely areas where food could be found such as lemmings and Arctic hares.

Instead, here there is no snow on the church path, but plenty of depressions in the gravel. The police, the paramedics, the journalists, Jon finds traces of their shoes, even the points of the camera tripod. He also finds a clump of bloody hair to the left of the path, not human and finer than that of a wolf. Jon studies it for a moment, lifts it to the light. He stands up, searching the path as he walks up to the church. He turns, sees the Falk farm in the distance, and the entrance to the field perhaps twenty metres away. Dust spirals higher than the trees in the field beyond Bo's farm, closer to Thyrup. Jon shields his eyes as he looks east. He lowers his hand as he turns, squints and holds his breath as he sees something loping across the field closest to the church.

If there is a den, then the wolf he sees in the field – for Jon knows it is a wolf – then the wolf might be returning to it. There is something in its mouth. *A hare, perhaps*, Jon thinks. He slips the bloody fur into his shirt pocket, and steps off the track. Jon skirts the dry-stone wall circling the church as he tracks the wolf from the hilltop. It disappears twice, re-emerging from the hedgerow as it crosses one field into the next. Jon smiles at the sight of the wolf, as it flicks long straight legs at an angle beneath its head, switching hind legs back and forth beneath its tail. It is a hare in the wolf's mouth, the long back legs and oversized ears are unmistakeable.

Jon stops as the wolf disappears for a third time. He waits, scans the hedgerows, the fields, but the wolf is gone.

Jon pulls a notebook from the cargo pocket of his shorts, searches for a pen, and finds the stub of an IKEA pencil. He checks his watch, makes some notes – description, size, direction. He pauses to sit on the ground, leans his back against the wall. The grass is stiff and prickly beneath his buttocks, pressing into his skin.

Just for a moment he is transported back to the *field* and he experiences a second or two of bliss, the kind he always feels when following and observing wolves in the wild. But it is only for a second, as his mobile rings, and Jon feels the energy drain from his body as he recognises the number.

"It's critical, Jon," Felix says, once they have discussed the situation. "The Prime Minister is very much involved. He wants your recommendation by the end of the day."

"It's Saturday," Jon says.

"That's right, and if we don't comment today then the story will simmer. By Monday morning Denmark will be awash with stories of hunters scouring the fields looking for wolves – man-eaters. Do you want that, Jon?"

"Of course not," Jon says, as he remembers the long thin case Sebastian slid into the back of the Land Rover.

"Then you had better give me your report – not just observations, but your conclusion. I need a definitive decision before this gets out of control. Do you understand?"

"Yes."

"I need you to advise me what to do about the wolves by lunchtime."

"That's in just a few hours."

"We need a comment ready for the evening news, Jon. Don't let me down."

Chapter 22

The dust from the field swirls around the old oak in the centre of the courtyard at the Falk family farm. It is older than the tractor and the equipment tucked inside the farm buildings, older than the cobbles pressed into the earth above its roots. It is older than Bo and his family, has lived longer than Bo's fathers and grandfathers. It has survived more than one drought by digging deep, drawing on the water buried deep down in the earth, below the farm, out of sight.

Jacob must dig deep if he is going to recover. Emma knows this, as she waits by the car as Camilla holds the passenger door open. His eyes are fixed on the farmhouse, but he doesn't move. Camilla beckons to Emma, stands back as she crouches beside Jacob.

"Come on," Emma says. "Let's go inside. Have something to eat."

Jacob says nothing and she takes his hand, squeezes it.

"Come with me."

The wind carries more than dust from the field. They can hear the steady drone and thrash of the combine harvester. The field was only half cut when they passed. Emma takes a chance. She leans close, slips her hand around Jacob's neck and whispers.

"Your dad's not here. He's not finished with the field. Come inside."

Jacob turns his head. His dull eyes flicker, just for a second, and he lifts one leg out of the car. Emma hears Camilla sigh, and she holds Jacob's hand, guides him out of the car and into the shade of the old oak. His mother walks on ahead. She has cold drinks on the table when they step inside the kitchen. She nods for Emma to take Jacob to the table.

The flies are more interested in the sugary drinks than Jacob is.

"The nurses said you had to drink more," Camilla says, clinging to the random theory that he is dehydrated, as if his listless behaviour is symptomatic of a simple lack of fluids.

Emma takes a sip of coke as Jacob leans back on the bench by the window. He looks over his shoulder and Emma follows his gaze to the aluminium shed at the bottom of the garden. She thinks it's strange that the farm, with all its neat lines, should have such an unkempt and abandoned patch of land behind the house, neglected, forgotten, full of weeds. They seem to flourish, tall and green between the broken yellow grasses. Jacob stares at the shed and the drone of the harvester stops, the wind drops, and the dust settles.

There is a car at the end of the driveway, close to the road. It raises a cloud of dust behind it as it approaches the farm.

"That's Bo," Camilla says.

The bench creaks as Jacob stiffens. Emma takes his hand.

"You have to go," he whispers.

"Go?" The word wrenches at her stomach, twisting like a knife. "I don't understand."

Jacob says nothing more. He pulls his hand free of Emma's as Bo enters the kitchen. His hair is brown, like the field, and the skin of his face is petaled with patches of brown, black where he has wiped at the sweat, white around his mouth. He places a dusty bottle of water on the kitchen counter and stares at Jacob.

"Feeling better?" he asks.

Jacob nods.

"Ready to work?"

"Not now, Bo," Camilla says.

"I could use some help in the field," he says, ignoring his wife.

"Maybe later," Jacob says.

Bo shifts his gaze to Emma, stares at her until Camilla touches his arm, and pushes a cup of coffee into his hand.

"Give them a minute, Bo," she says.

Bo leans against the counter, watching his son and the girl over the rim of the mug as he drinks. Emma's stomach twists into a spiral, tighter than ever, and then Jacob speaks, and the spiral becomes a knot. It burns as it tightens.

"I want to talk to the police," he says, his voice trembles.

"What?" Camilla says.

Bo takes another sip of coffee, his eyes locked on his son.

"It's the right thing to do, dad."

"I'll tell you what's right and wrong," Bo says.

"Bo?" Camilla dips her head towards Emma. "We've got company."

"He wants to talk," Bo says. "He could have waited until she was gone, but he wants her to hear it. Is that right, son?"

Emma shifts on the bench and Jacob takes her hand.

"Come on, Jacob. I'm listening. We're all listening," he says, and glares at Emma.

"I think I should go," she says.

Emma lets go of Jacob and slides along the bench. She stands up, her breath falters for a second, and she takes a step towards the door, between Bo and the table.

"No," Bo says. "I don't think so."

Emma cries out as Bo grips her arm and thrusts her into the seat opposite Jacob. Camilla grabs his hand and he slaps her in the face. She reels into the kitchen. The table rocks as Jacob stands up.

"Sit down, son."

"Dad…"

"I said sit down," Bo shouts. He slams his palm on the table. "All of you, around the table." Bo grips his wife's shoulder and presses her onto the bench beside Jacob. He pushes Emma's chair closer to the table, pinning her stomach against the edge. "Right. You want to talk, then let's talk," he says. "But I'll start."

There is dust on the table, an outline of Bo's hand, and Emma stares at it. She thinks about her mobile in her pocket, thinks about her father, and then places her hands in her lap as Bo reaches for a can of coke, pops the tab, and takes a long drink. He places it, quietly, on the table.

"There's blood on this farm," he says, and looks at Jacob. "Your grandfather's, grandmother's, mine, Camilla's, even yours. You remember when you cut your hand on the tractor this spring? It was a bloody mess. Then there was the knife in the barn, when you cut the bailing twine. You were only nine at the time. Your blood, on the knife, on the hay, your clothes, my clothes. Our blood is in this earth, Jacob. It's Falk earth, Falk blood. It's part of farm life, it's part of our bond to the earth. But, this year, the earth is too dry to take our blood. It just dries and flakes at the surface. There's no bonding this year, son, the earth is too dry. The only thing that keeps living is that bloody oak," he says, and points at it. "It's the only thing surviving this summer. Do you know why?" Bo takes a sip of coke, wipes his mouth with the back of his hand, smears the dust across his cheek. "I'll tell you why. It's the only thing digging deep enough. We have to dig deep, all of us, if we are going to survive this summer. We have to do difficult things, things that seem wrong. Things we would never do. But we have to. We have to do these things. We're dead if we don't."

"Bo," Camilla says. "You're scaring them. You're scaring me."

"Good. We all need to be scared. We all need to dig deep."

Emma presses her fingers into her pocket. She can feel the slim case of her mobile, smooth against her fingertips.

"Now, the priest told me something this morning, and I need to know if it's true," Bo says.

Emma freezes, and the knot tightens.

"To be honest, I can't really believe it, but," he says, and shrugs. "If the priest says it is so. It must be true. Isn't that right, Emma?"

"What?"

"You told him something, didn't you?"

"He's a priest." She looks at Jacob. "He shouldn't have said anything."

Jacob's eyes widen, and he swallows, flicks his gaze from Emma to his father. "It was a secret," he whispers.

"Secrets and lies, son. You remember what Aage said about werewolves? How they lived and moved among us? Well it's true, isn't it?" Bo smoothes his hand through Emma's hair until he has it bunched in his fist. She cries out when he twists it to one side. "Just think, they burned werewolves at the stake back then."

He twists again. Emma cries out, and Jacob leaps at his father, scattering the coke cans as he lunges, fists swinging. Bo hurls Emma against the kitchen counter, glances at her at the sound of her head striking the cupboards, and then reels as Jacob lands a punch on the side of his head.

"Jacob," Camilla shouts.

Bo takes another punch, a third to his stomach, and then he lifts his head, sharply, clips Jacob's chin, and, as Jacob staggers, he grabs his shoulders, slams him into the wall, and presses his head against the photo of the farm, as he squeezes dust-caked, farm-beaten fingers around his son's throat.

"You know where they are," he shouts, spittle flecking Jacob's face. "All this time, you knew. We could have killed those fucking wolves, been done with them. But no, you had to keep that little secret, saving it for someone special." Bo twists Jacob's head to look at Emma. "Is she special? Eh? Does she mean more to you than your mother, than this farm? More than me?" Bo bangs Jacob's head against the photo frame. The glass cracks and he shouts. "Answer me, son."

Emma stirs on the floor, presses her hands against the flagstones, and turns as Jacob stares at her, spit bubbling on his lips as Bo squeezes his throat. She pulls her mobile from her pocket. Bo sees it and shouts at Camilla.

"Take it. Take her phone."

"Let him go," she says. "Let my son go and I'll

take it."

Bo steps back and Jacob slides down the wall to the floor. Camilla smoothes her hand against Emma's cheek and takes her mobile. Emma crawls around the kitchen counter towards Jacob. She reaches for him as Bo grabs her by the hair, pulls her to her feet, and marches her out of the farmhouse.

"Stay down, boy," Bo says, as he twists Emma across the cobblestones and around the back of the house. She cries out, stumbling as he grips her hair and pushes her across the rough ground, past the thistles and weeds, over the rubble and into the shed. "You'll stay here until I'm done."

"Don't hurt him," Emma says, as Bo shoves her onto the floor.

"No?"

"He's your son."

"He's a stupid boy, pretending to be a man. Now, thanks to you, he gets to grow up."

The light disappears as Bo shuts the shed door and Emma screams.

"There's water in the bucket. You'd better drink. It's going to be a hot day."

She hears the snick of a bolt as Bo locks the shed door. The walls are hot; they burn her fingers, the floor is musty, sticky with pellets and something that smells like urine. Emma scuffs her knees as she gets to her feet. She pounds on the shed door, kicks at it, and it moves, until Bo shouts at her, and slides a second bolt into position at the bottom of the door. Each kick rattles around the shed, vibrating and shuddering through her foot, through her body, and into her head. Her screams hurt her ears, and the dust, the stale air, the splinters and the shavings of wood catch in her throat, prick at her tongue, and she slides to the floor, hugs her knees to her chest and cries.

Emma's tears splash onto her wrists, as she sweats and shakes inside the stifling metal shed, beneath the sun of Denmark's hottest summer on record. She thinks of her dad, cries for him to help her, she calls out for him, but she hears only the sound of her own voice, barely recognising it as her words rasp from her throat in the dust and the heat. She calls again, until the words are too sticky, and her tongue too dry to speak. It is quiet then, and she is left alone with her thoughts and fears, alone like a beast in a shed.

Chapter 23

The irony is not lost on Aage. The wolves crossed the border from Germany into Denmark, and the first man to be killed by the wolves is German. The family is destroyed by their loss. The police brought them to Aage once the counsellors had tried to console them. The church, it seems, is where they will find comfort, and Aage welcomes them with quiet words, a soft touch. He shows them into his office, whispers to the police that they can go, and makes a cup of coffee. The man's son is more interested in the wooden chest of toys, and Aage encourages him with a smile. The boy builds with LEGO bricks, as the daughter clings to her mother, and Aage serves coffee and cold drinks. This is not the time to be impatient, but he has an interview scheduled with Lærke Wang and he thinks about what he is going to say on his first TV spot since the wolves arrived in Thyrup. The German woman shakes as she reaches for her coffee, and Aage takes her hand as he sits down. She glances at the wall, and he imagines her to be looking at the place where her husband was attacked, the place where he died.

"It's a tragedy," he says, speaking German, the language of the majority in Thyrup each summer, the language of his extended flock.

"My husband was looking for a night-time cache," she says. "A *Geocache*, something you find with an app on your phone."

"Yes," Aage says, as he remembers a German family asking if they could leave one along the path a few years ago.

"The night caches have reflectors, so that you can

find them."

"And he liked doing that? That was his hobby?"

"Yes," she whispers, and looks at her son. "He was going to take him with him, but I said no. Just think…"

This is what he will tell Lærke in the interview. It seems that the politicians are blind to the human cost in the wolf debate. Blind to compensation and the fear of the wolf, but they cannot turn a blind eye at a death. Aage holds the mother's hand as the daughter plays with her brother. He makes another cup of coffee, arranges for a taxi when she is ready to leave, and promises to mention her husband in his Sunday sermon, the next morning.

"I will come to the service," she says. "Before we leave for Germany."

"I would like that," Aage says.

He walks with the family to their car, steers the mother away from the path, and waits until they have driven away. He has thirty minutes before his interview.

Aage's shoes crunch in the gravel as he walks between the tombstones to pick up his car keys from the office. He takes the back door, squints in the glare of the sun against the white church walls and stops at the sound of whimpering. He looks around, tilts his head and turns to locate the sound. A second whimper, quieter than the last, leads him to the door of the tool shed at the back of the church. The door opens, and Aage's breath catches in his throat at the sight of the dog, bound, bloody, and gasping behind the lawn mower.

"Bo," Aage whispers, as he enters the shed and shuts the door.

It is a pitiful sight. Aage is moved perhaps more than he imagined he might be. He struggles with the thought that this is the *wolf* that killed the German man on the church path, but he knows it must be. Bo never mentioned it when they talked, never said that he had hidden a killer on church ground. Aage is almost angry, but the sight of the dog – a domestic dog – softens his thoughts, and he finds water and a bowl, loosens the oily rag tied around the dog's muzzle, and helps it drink, holding the bowl as it laps at the water with a stiff, dry tongue.

Aage finds another rope, a little frayed but strong when he tests it, and ties one end around the dog's neck. He loops and ties the other end around the steering wheel on the lawn mower, a small tractor, barely used this summer. Aage loosens the knots around the dog's legs and it twitches onto its stomach. Aage takes a chance, smoothes his hand through the dog's fur, and pulls softly at its ears. He knows he should kill and bury it, before it is found, but the thought is too much, and, a quick look at his watch, suggests he doesn't have the time. Aage pours more water into the bowl and leaves the dog in the shed. He spends a moment outside, looking for a bolt, patting his pocket for a key, and then settles on dragging a concrete slab against the bottom of the door. He hurries to his office, collects his keys and thinks no more of the dog as he drives down the road for his interview.

The sight of his son surprises him when he enters the sports hall. Jon is standing beside Anton and the look on his son's face troubles him.

"You should be resting," Aage says, as he shakes his son's hand.

"It hurts to lie down," he says.

"But what are you doing here?"

"Telling the truth."

"About what?" Aage looks at Jon. "Did he put you up to this?"

Anton stiffens at a stab of pain in his ribs. "It was a dog," he says, and points at Lærke and the camera crew fiddling with a tripod. "I've told them."

"How could you? A man has died, Anton. How could you lie?"

"How could *you*? You're a priest, father, or had you forgotten."

"This man," Aage says, as he points at Jon, "has no experience of wolves in Denmark. He has only seen them in Greenland. They are not the same."

"How would you know?" Jon asks.

"I *know* what I have seen. I listen to what people tell me. Your daughter, for example."

"What?"

"The wolves' den. Has she told you where it is yet? She's been there a couple of times. It was supposed to be their secret, but nothing is secret now, is it? Not now that a man has been killed."

"She told you where it is?"

"Not in so many words," Aage says. He smiles at the look on Jon's face.

"What have you done?" Anton asks his father, as Jon steps to one side and takes his mobile from his pocket.

"Nothing."

"Did you tell Bo about the den?"

"I told him this morning."

"That's convenient."

"There's nothing convenient about a man dying,

Anton. But the fact that there are wolves in the area, close to the church is *interesting*, it's more than a coincidence." He points at Lærke. "I will tell her what I know. The people and the politicians will decide if it is convenient or not. But, by then, who knows? Maybe everything will have sorted itself out. Perhaps it will all be over."

"What about the dog?" Anton asks, as Aage walks away. "Are you going to tell them about that too?"

"There is no dog," Aage says. "You were trampled by a herd of cattle. It's no wonder you can't remember what you saw. I'm surprised you can remember your name." Aage taps the side of his head. "It's not just your ribs that were damaged."

Aage sees Jon frown at his mobile, and brushes past him on the way to his interview.

In the interview Lærke forgets the rigid objectivism she is famous for. Her words are soft, like Aage's own, as they talk about the tragic incident by the church, and Aage paints a picture of a family man, enjoying an activity shared by many across the world.

"He could never have known that he would be the victim of a vicious, merciless attack by a wild animal. Why do the politicians not act? Why do they let this predator roam around our countryside, in our back gardens, between our houses, kindergartens, even our churches, unchecked? How many more people must die in the jaws of the wolf before Christiansborg reacts, and the Prime Minister protects his people. I am a humble man," Aage says. "I do what I can within the law set by the government and by God. I will walk the woods and paths of Thyrup with anyone afraid to do so, local or tourist, just as I know many people in this caring, tight-knit community will do. But we are few, the majority are frightened and with good cause. A man was killed in the early hours of the morning, while out for a peaceful walk, enjoying the cooler hours before the heat of the sun. I don't think anyone would have ever imagined he would not eat breakfast with his family today, or ever again, because of a wolf."

Aage looks for Jon at the end of his interview, but the wolf biologist is gone. There will be no counter argument. Aage thinks it is just as well. He likes Jon. It would be a shame to see him take the wrong side in such a simple closed-case as this one.

Aage smokes during his drive back to the church. A simple pleasure, a reward at the end of busy day. He parks his car and pinches the end of the cigarette, careful not to throw the stub into the dry grass, pushing it inside the packet instead.

He sweats in the sun. His collar is damp. The breeze that so often comes from the sea is absent. There is not a cloud in the sky, and the sun bakes the ground for another day in a string of scorching days. Aage thinks of the cold beer in his fridge, but it is too early to drink. He wonders if Camilla has more of her strawberry buttermilk, but the thought reminds him of the dog in the shed and the milk sours in his mind, in the heat, outside the church on the hilltop. Aage walks through the cemetery and around the back of the church.

The shed door is ajar, the concrete slab lies flat on the gravel. The hairs on the back of Aage's neck prickle as he looks around the gravestones. The swallows dive unperturbed from nests tucked behind the gutters in the church roof as Aage takes a slow step towards the shed door. He opens it wide, sees the wet fibres of the rope on the floor and the end dangling from the lawn mower. Aage swears under his breath and takes out his mobile.

"Where are you?" he asks when Bo answers. "I need you here, at the church."

"I'm busy," Bo says. "I have a field to harvest."

"Forget the harvest, your bloody dog is loose, Bo."

"What dog?"

"Don't be stupid. The one you tied up in the church shed. *That* dog. Do you remember now?"

"I remember you telling me to get a dog. You gave me a print out with the dog's details on it. It's as much your dog as it is mine. And, if you say it has escaped from the church shed, what business is it of mine?"

"What business is it?"

"I suggest you find your dog before it gets dark. You never know what might happen."

"Listen, Bo, you need to find this dog. Send Jacob to help me at the very least."

"Jacob and I are busy."

"Doing what?"

"You don't need to know."

"You're going after the wolves?" Aage pauses at the thought. "Of course, if you produce them now, if you kill them…"

"I will get a fine at the most."

"You'll be a hero."

Bo makes a sound that Aage thinks might be a laugh, but he is not sure.

"I just want the chance to save something of the summer," Bo says.

Chapter 24

The road to the Falk farm is thick with traffic, blocked by police cars, and there are fire trucks in the fields. A wall of smoke cuts across the gravel road, and there is an ambulance parked at the entrance. Jon bumps his Toyota along the grass verge until the police wave him to a stop.

"You can't go any further."

"My daughter is at the farm."

"No," the policeman says. "There's no-one at the farm. We got them off in time."

"In time?"

"Before the fire got too close to the house."

Jon puts the car into first gear and accelerates around the police road block, ignoring shouts from the policeman. He sees Camilla with the paramedics and parks beside the ambulance. He leaves the door open and the engine running.

"She can't speak," the paramedic says and stops Jon with a flat hand against his chest. "Smoke inhalation."

"Camilla," Jon says, pushing past the paramedic. "Where's Emma?" He leans forward as Camilla tugs the oxygen mask from her face.

"Bo," Camilla whispers, her words lost in the crackle of flames just a few hundred metres away.

"He's got Emma?"

"He took her away," Camilla says and coughs.

"That's enough," the paramedic says. He shoves Jon to one side and tugs the mask back over Camilla's nose and mouth.

Jon runs for the car. He knows where exactly where Emma is.

He slams the door and accelerates down the gravel drive. The smoke envelops the Toyota, restricting Jon's vision to the dashboard, the wipers, and bright orange flames as he bursts through a wall of fire. The heat cracks the glass and the tyres blister as Jon accelerates. The flames burn a path through the smoke and Jon sees the oak tree, a burning effigy of black boughs in the centre of the courtyard. Jon drives on, bumping the Toyota past the flames to the rough ground behind the farmhouse.

The fire is contained for the moment within the buildings, and Jon runs to the shed shouting Emma's name. He throws back the bolts and pulls the handle, but a rusty padlock and chain prevents the door from opening more than a hand's width. He crouches at the door and reaches through the gap.

"Emma?"

Jon flinches at a loud *crump*, as something explodes in the courtyard, and then he feels it, a soft, warm touch of skin on his hand, and he almost pulls his daughter through the gap.

"Dad."

"I'm here. I'm going to get you out."

"It's locked."

"I know," he says. "I have to let go. I have to find something to open the lock."

The windows of the farmhouse burst and glass shatters onto the rough patch of garden. Thick smoke billows out of the kitchen.

Jon finds nothing by the shed. If there are any tools to break the lock, Jon knows they will be in the farm buildings, the ones blazing and popping in the heat of the fire.

"Emma," he says. "Stay on this side of the shed."

"What are you going to do?"

"Stay flat against the wall."

"Dad?"

Jon runs back to the Toyota, thrusts it into first gear and bumps it over the rubble. He strikes the side of the shed, lifting the wall from its foundation, but not enough to break the aluminium sides from the bolts securing it in place. Jon curses as the tyres pop and the car stalls. The shed lists to one side, and Jon crawls to the space beneath the wall. More windows shatter, and he has to shout above the roar of the flames.

"You have to crawl under, Emma, under the wall."

"I can't," she says, as she flattens her stomach against the stone floor. "It's still too low."

Jon grabs an old rake lying on the ground. The shaft breaks as he levers it against the wall. Emma cries out as Jon throws his shoulder against the shed side. It gives a little. He takes a run, hurls himself at the shed, coughing in a drift of smoke, and then runs again, and again, until Emma has her shoulders wedged under the side of the shed, and Jon grabs the rough aluminium in his hands. The metal slices into his palms as he lifts, splashing drops of blood onto Emma's dusty shirt until she squirms free of the shed, coughs in the dust and smoke, and clings to her father as he pulls her close.

"The den," she coughs. "That's where they've gone."

"And you know where it is?"

"Yes."

Emma grips her father's hand as they skirt around the smoke and across the field. The roar of the flames licking at the roof of the farmhouse, biting into the farm buildings, and crisping the bark of the oak, fills the air. They choke as the smoke threatens to fill their lungs, ducking as they run, seeking the fresher, cooler air, all the way to the entrance to the Holloway. Emma lets go of Jon's hand at the bramble entrance.

"Emma, wait."

"It's this way."

"I know, but I need to look at you. Stop for a second."

The smoke obscures the sun, casting a grey ethereal light across Emma's face. Jon sees the tracks of tears running down her cheeks, wipes dirt from her mouth, and brushes grit from around her eyes. They are brighter than ever, urgent.

"Dad."

"Just a second."

"We have to go."

"No," he says. "I have to get you away."

"They are going after the wolves. We have to stop them."

"Emma…"

"It's my fault, dad. If I hadn't told the priest, if I had just kept it secret…"

"It's all right, Emma. It's not your fault."

"He's going to kill them. I won't let him."

Emma slips away from her father and darts into the tunnel. Jon follows, the brambles clinging to his shirt, scratching at his scalp. He can see Emma, just in front of him. He pulls free from the brambles and crawls after her. She stops him before the end of the tunnel, and he slides onto his belly and squirms the last few metres.

"They've got guns," Emma whispers, and she takes her father's hand.

"Stay here," Jon says.

Jon crawls out of the tunnel, ignoring the scratch and prick of the thorns. He heaves his leg forwards and tumbles onto the small patch of open ground in front of the bunker. The smoke light catches Bo and Jon sees the rifle in his hand.

"Get up," Bo says, and jerks the end of the rifle towards the bunker.

"Bo…"

"Over there." Bo pushes Jon against the wall. The concrete is old, blistered with pits and pockmarks, covered in ivy, brown and green, the roots are deep, hidden like the foundations of the bunker.

"Dad?"

"Find the girl," Bo says, and points at the brambles covering the Holloway.

"Run, Emma," Jon shouts, and Bo clips him across the head with the barrel of the rifle.

Jon hears Jacob shout something. He argues with his father, until Bo pushes him through the brambles and Jacob is gone.

"The den is empty," Bo says. "But there's plenty of spoor. They were here. Recently." He pushes the barrel of the rifle into Jon's ribs. "You're the expert. Where would they go?"

"Away from the fire," Jon says.

He looks up as Jacob crawls out of the brambles.

"She's gone, dad."

"Because you let her," Bo says, and thrusts the rifle into Jacob's hands. "Carry this. We have to hunt them now."

"You'll never find them," Jon says. "There's too much smoke, and it'll be dark soon. They are long gone."

Bo grabs Jon's shirt at the neck and pulls him to his feet. "We have to find them. Don't you understand? They have to die, tonight."

"That's enough, Bo. Stop, look over there. Your farm is burning. You have to forget about the wolves, save your family…" Jon looks at the entrance to the den, just as a shadow appears in the crack in the concrete. The face is boxy, fox-like, but fatter with thicker ears. "You said the den was empty?"

"I thought it was," Bo says, as he lets go of Jon's shirt.

He turns his head at the sound of a low growl.

"That's the mother," Jacob says.

"You're going to have to shoot it, son."

"No dad."

"Then give me the rifle."

A belch of smoke pushes through the hedgerow and the brambles. It clings to the trees hiding the bunker, quilts the ground with a soft pillow of grey and hides the wolf. Jon swallows as he presses himself against the wall of the bunker and straightens his back. The wolf growls again, but it is another man with a shotgun creeping out of the brambles that turns Jon's head as Sebastian points his gun at Bo.

"Leave," he says. "Now."

"Who are you?"

"Your wife didn't tell you? We warned her this would happen, that your farm would burn if you didn't leave the wolves alone."

"You set fire to my farm?"

"We warned you."

"You bastard," Bo says. He runs at Sebastian, reaches out to grab the barrel, but stops at the crack of a single gunshot. Jon sees the wolf pounce on the cub; grip the fur at the back of its neck between its teeth, and dart away into the undergrowth. The smoke follows as if sucked away in the lupine vacuum. Jon imagines, for a second, the wolves moving the cubs from the den, carrying them across the fields, only to stop at the sound of a man dying, gasping for his last breath, the air sucking and bubbling through the bloody hole in his chest.

Bo takes the rifle from Jacob's hand and pulls his son to his chest, turning him away from the man bleeding to death in the brambles. Jon scrambles past them, and crouches at Sebastian's side. The shotgun is cradled in the man's lap and Jon moves it.

"He's going to need help," he says. "We have to get him out of here."

Bo nods and reaches for his mobile. Jon searches for something to press into the hole in Sebastian's chest.

"I need something to stop the blood," he says.

Jacob slips free of his father and pulls his t-shirt over his head. The light in his eyes flickers as he tears the cloth into rough strips. Jon packs them into the wound.

"He was going to shoot my dad," he says.

"They're sending an ambulance," Bo says, as he slips his phone into his pocket. "We have to get him into the field or they'll never find us."

"That way," Jon says. "We'll follow the wolf."

Sebastian groans as the three men carry him into the field. The lights of the ambulance bump across the furrows. Jon blinks in the blue swirl of emergency lights. He looks away, and across the field, he sees a figure running. Jon knows it is his daughter, he recognises her shadow and her voice as she shouts for help. He looks behind her and sees a great black shape, its colour hidden in the shadows and smoke, but nothing hides its intent as it closes on Emma.

Jon grabs the rifle out of Jacob's hands, pulls the stock to his chest, and drifts the sight in front of the beast. He pulls the trigger, curses, and chambers a round into the barrel. He aims again, shoots and misses, only startling the beast. But it is enough to give Emma a head start to the hedgerow. Jon starts to run as the ambulance stops beside them.

"Wait," Bo shouts, as Jacob runs after Jon.

But Jacob ignores him, and soon the two men are pounding across the field, chasing the beast that is chasing Emma towards the church at the top of the hill. It stands tall and white in the dying light above the smoke and flames burning in the fields below.

Chapter 25

Emma sees the church shining in the retreating twilight. Her chest burns as she runs, but she won't stop, not until she reaches the church. She has to get inside, and it's the only building around. She doesn't think about sanctuary, on sacred ground. She has no thoughts for werewolves or wolf-mongering, all she knows is that she is being chased and she will die if she doesn't run.

She heard the rifle shots. The second one was louder, closer. It slowed the beast chasing her.

She doesn't say wolf, but the thought is there. This is the beast of beasts, the greatest predator in the whole of Denmark, perhaps even Scandinavia. But she has other thoughts too, as she remembers the smell of piss in the shed, the chain, and the dog food. Jacob never said anything about dogs, but her dad has talked about them the whole time.

"It's not a wolf," he says. "It's a dog."

Emma reaches the edge of the field and risks a glance over her shoulder. She sees it then, bounding towards her, great claws scratching at the earth, teeth bared, jaws wide. Her senses are sharpened through fear, and she sees the saliva fleeing the beast's maw, can almost hear it slapping against the earth in great blobs of slather and drool. And then she runs.

There is a path winding up to the church. She might even make it. The thought keeps her going, keeps her running, even when her thighs begin to burn and her chest aches with the force of breathing, running, screaming. She can't scream anymore, all she can do is run.

If she doesn't run, she dies. She knows it.

The church is just there. White on a black hilltop. And there is a light, and Emma cries, tears but no sound, as she sees the light bob towards her. It is a torch. Someone is coming, and she almost slows, but the scrabble and click of the beast's claws on the gravel urges her on.

"Emma?" Aage says, as he walks down the path. "Is that you?"

"Run," she says. She can't know that Jacob said the same to another man at almost the same time, on the same path. Wolves, her father would say, have a territory, and if she had the energy to think of such things, she would realise that wild dogs are no different. And she was in its territory.

Emma collides with the priest, and they tumble to the gravel path. She is the first to stand as the beast thunders up the path and sinks its teeth into the priest's leg. Emma grabs Aage's arm, and tries to pull him up the path, away from the beast.

She can see it now, its thick fur matted and bloody, a frayed rope loose around its neck. It growls as it bites through the priest's trouser leg, pressing and biting with broken and bloody teeth. Aage screams and drops his torch, and the light rolls in an arc down the path, casting a triangle of yellow light onto black eyes and bloody teeth.

Emma lets go of the priest's arm, and kicks at the dog, kicking its head, forcing it to one side. But it won't let go. She kicks it again, grabs it by the tail, cries as she pulls it and the dog pulls the priest, and together the three of them inch their way down the path, away from the church and away from sanctuary.

The dog has had enough, and Emma flies onto her back, as the dog lets go of the priest and leaps onto Emma. She presses her arm into its mouth, screaming as the dog clamps and bites, tears, and shakes at her bare arm, bloody now, the skin ragged.

Emma cries out for the priest to help her, but as he limps to his feet, he chooses to run instead and she hears the click of gravel beneath his feet. Blood is in her eyes, it is in her mouth, and the pain, it's like fire and a vice, and there is no stopping it. She screams again, and the beast finally lets go. She opens her eyes, sees it rear its head back, sees it lunge for another bite as a bullet whistles over her head and snaps the beast's head back. The body lands heavy on her legs. And then Jacob is there, pulling the dog off her body. He kneels on it, as the dog chokes a last breath before it is finished, and all that remains of the beast is the blood on Jacob's chest, the ragged flesh on Emma's arm, and the lifeless, pitiful dog dead on the gravel path just metres from the entrance to the churchyard.

Jon lowers the rifle, handing it to Jacob as he kneels next to his daughter and examines Emma's arm in the yellow glow of the priest's lamplight.

Emma's breathing is as ragged as the flesh on her arm. Jon removes his shirt, wraps it around the wound and cinches it tight. Emma leans her head on his chest and closes her eyes, just for a second. In that second she is at peace, and the terror of the shed, the flames, and the beast is over. But when she opens her eyes, she realises the nightmare has just begun, and she is powerless to stop it. She can't speak, can't say the words to stop Jacob from pressing the barrel of his father's rifle into the soft flesh beneath his chin. She can't scream for him to stop, can't even breathe as her lungs stop working, and she is captured in the priest's light, caught in the horror of the last seconds of Jacob's life, as he holds the rifle with one hand, and presses the trigger with his thumb.

Jon snaps his head around to see Jacob fall to the ground. The rifle slaps onto Jacob's chest and skitters onto the gravel. His daughter's cries are drowned by the wail of the man running up the path, screaming that it can't be, that his son is not lying on the path with a rifle by his side and blood, bone and brain in the gravel.

"He's not dead," Bo says, as he cradles his son's head in his hands. "You're not dead," he says, and he drags Jacob's body into his lap and twists his fingers through the long, black surfer hair, the innocent locks of a young man caught up in a stupid, senseless game of fear and politics. "My son is not dead," Bo says, as he stares at Jon, waiting for him to nod, to tell him that it isn't so, that Jacob is not dead.

Jon lifts Emma onto her feet, presses her head to his chest, and walks her past the two Falk men, one dead, the other dying on the path below the church. For grief is a kind of death when you realise that, all of a sudden, you are alone, and *nothing* will bring that person back.

There are lights swirling around the car park, and Jon realises that the priest must have called an ambulance and the police, a busy night in Thyrup. The television crews are there already and the night has been dubbed *the night of the wolf*. Jon looks up at the moon, expecting a full moon, instead there is just a sliver. The paramedics, the same team from the fields below, pull him to one side, as they take care of his daughter.

Jon waits outside the ambulance, waits until they lay Emma down on the stretcher, slip an oxygen mask over her mouth and inject morphine into her arm. They dress the wound, and he steps inside the ambulance to stroke her hair as she closes her eyes.

They can save her arm, he is sure. She will wear long sleeves for a while, he thinks, but the scars will remind her of Jacob each and every night until they can begin to forget the wolf summer.

Jon gives a statement to the police. He is tempted to talk with Bo when they are finished with him, but there is something he must do. Jon beckons to Lærke.

"Can we talk with you?" she asks. "Is your daughter alright?"

"This way," he says. "And bring your camera."

The church door is locked. Jon walks around the side and the cameraman follows. He finds a side door, tests it, kicks it open, and bursts inside Aage's office to find the priest dousing his leg in medicinal spirits. Jon slaps the bottle off the table and it smashes on the floor. The camera captures everything, and Lærke steps to one side as Jon lifts the priest from his chair and presses him against the wall.

"I will shout for the police," Aage says.

"Go ahead."

"What do you want? Why are *they* here?"

"This is your confession," Jon says. He points at the camera. "You're going to make things right. And then, you're going to resign."

"My duty is to God and to my congregation," Aage says. "Who will watch over my flock if I leave them? Who will protect them from the wolf?"

"You can't protect them from the wolf. You can't even protect them from yourself." Jon turns to the camera. "Ask him about the dog," he says. "Ask him how he sacrificed Bo Falk, how he forced him on a path that took three lives and split a whole community. Ask him that, and then ask him how many times, and how many people have actually *seen* a wolf, or have they just seen their shepherd – the sheep in wolf's clothing."

Jon leaves the priest's office. There is a light on in the tool shed, and the ends of a frayed rope trailing out of the door. He shouts at a policeman circling the grounds and points at the door as he walks to the parking area.

Anton sits in the passenger seat of his pickup. He waves at Jon and points at his wife as she holds Camilla tight. Bo is close by, but the handcuffs around his wrists stop him from holding anyone. A policewoman helps Bo into the back of the patrol car as Jon walks to the ambulance.

Jon holds Emma's hand on the drive to the hospital. Her grip is strong despite the drugs and it gives him hope. His mobile rings and Jon fumbles it into his left hand.

"You were supposed to contact me," Felix says.

"You've seen the news? Seen the farm burning?"

"Yes. They say a girl has been attacked."

"My daughter."

"Jon, I'm so sorry."

"Just listen, Felix," Jon says, pausing as the ambulance accelerates around a TV van. "I have two recommendations. Education and compensation, comprehensive, both of them. There is a good veterinarian in the area. With the right support, I think she will become an excellent judge to determine if a dog or a wolf has killed livestock. You can use Thyrup as a test case. She can help me with the education programme."

"What's that, Jon?"

"I'm staying, Felix. I'll commute from Copenhagen, maybe stay at the beach house once a week. But I can't leave."

"Why don't you sleep on it? We can talk next week."

"The wolves are here now, Felix. You sent me here to study them, but all I ended up doing was studying the people. I became part of the problem. I told you to send a psychologist."

"Yes, you did.

"But you sent a biologist, and I need to get in the field. The wolves are here, I don't need to go to Greenland for a while."

"If you're sure?"

"I need to get started."

Lærke's report was part of the breaking news being broadcast across the country. Jon catches the latest developments in the hospital lounge as he waits for the nurses to dress Emma's wound. They assure him it will heal, but he knows the real wounds are deeper, and for those he will need help.

He pulls out his phone and dials his wife's number.

"Elin," he says, when she answers. "I need your help."

Emma once told him that wolves tore their family apart, now, Jon hopes, they might bring them together.

PAINT THE DEVIL

Author's Note

The wolf debate continues in Denmark, and in every country where wolves and their territories are disputed. The question I ask myself – especially since writing *Paint the Devil* – is if I would think differently if I had children, or if I was a farmer, a hunter, a pet-owner. I don't have an answer, only a gut-feeling that wolves belong in our world as much as we belong in theirs. I spent two months on the Yukon River, in a party of four adults and two children under the age of ten. We travelled through wolf and bear country armed with nothing more than bear spray and the hope that we made enough noise to keep any large predators at bay. We saw plenty of wolf tracks and plenty of bears, some at close quarters. It was exhilarating, not frightening. We were called irresponsible; others thought we were lucky, I like to think we were respectful.

There are a lot of good books on the subject of wolves and people, presenting both sides of the story, even that of the wolf, in as far as it is possible. To the reader curious to learn more about the wolf and the history of human interaction, I would suggest the following books:

Of Wolves and Men, by Barry Lopez and
The Company of Wolves, by Peter Steinhart

I saw my first wolf in the wild in Denali National Park, Alaska, a few weeks after we got off the river. I won't forget it, and I can't wait to see another, maybe even in Denmark, because despite what we humans may think or do, the wolf is here to stay, during or after our lifetime.

Chris
October 2018
Denmark

PAINT THE DEVIL

Acknowledgements

I would like to thank Isabel Dennis-Muir for her invaluable editing skills and feedback on the manuscript, and biologist Jørgen Møller for his support and comments. While several people have contributed to *Paint the Devil*, the mistakes and inaccuracies are all my own.

Chris
October 2018
Denmark

About the Author

Christoffer Petersen is the author's pen name. He lives in Denmark. Chris started writing stories about Greenland while teaching in Qaanaaq, the largest village in the very north of Greenland – the population peaked at 600 during the two years he lived there. Chris spent a total of seven years in Greenland, teaching in remote communities and at the Police Academy in the capital of Nuuk.

Chris continues to be inspired by the vast icy wilderness of the Arctic and his books have a common setting in the region, with a Scandinavian influence. He has also watched enough Bourne movies to no longer be surprised by the plot, but not enough to get bored.

You can find Chris in Denmark or online here:

www.christoffer-petersen.com

PAINT THE DEVIL

By the same Author

THE GREENLAND CRIME SERIES
featuring Constable David Maratse

SEVEN GRAVES, ONE WINTER Book 1
BLOOD FLOE Book 2
WE SHALL BE MONSTERS Book 3

Short Stories from the same series

KATABATIC
CONTAINER
TUPILAQ
THE LAST FLIGHT
THE HEART THAT WAS A WILD GARDEN

THE GREENLAND TRILOGY
featuring Konstabel Fenna Brongaard

THE ICE STAR Book 1
IN THE SHADOW OF THE MOUNTAIN Book 2
THE SHAMAN'S HOUSE Book 3

THE POLARPOL ACTION THRILLERS
featuring Sergeant Petra "Piitalaat" Jensen and more

NORTHERN LIGHT Book 1

THE DETECTIVE FREJA HANSEN SERIES
set in Denmark and Scotland

FELL RUNNER Introductory novella

PAINT THE DEVIL

THE SIRIUS SLEDGE PATROL
featuring Oversergent Mikael Gregersen and more

PITERAQ Story 1

MADE IN DENMARK
short stories *featuring* Milla Moth set in Denmark

DANISH DESIGN Story 1

THE WHEELMAN SHORTS
short stories *featuring* Noah Lee set in Australia

PULP DRIVER Story 1

THE DARK ADVENT SERIES
featuring Police Commissioner Petra "Piitalaat" Jensen
set in Greenland

THE CALENDAR MAN Book 1
THE TWELFTH NIGHT Book 2

30886919R00129

Printed in Poland
by Amazon Fulfillment
Poland Sp. z o.o., Wrocław